Tuesday
06 28-22
Douglas Li
13 & Homan
7-7

1

She BRINGS THE WORST KIND

GINA WEST

ARE YOU ON OUR EMAIL
LIST?

SIGN UP ON OUR WEBSITE

www.thecartelpublications.com

OR TEXT THE WORD:

CARTELBOOKS TO 22828

FOR PRIZES, CONTESTS, ETC.

CHECK OUT OTHER TITLES BY THE CARTEL PUBLICATIONS

4

WWW.THECARTELPUBLICATIONS.COM

SHE BRINGS THE WORST KIND

BY

GINA WEST

Library of Congress Control Number: 2017952904

ISBN 10: 1945240237

ISBN 13: 978-1945240232

Cover Design: Cover Design: Bookslutgirl.com

www.thecartelpublications.com
First Edition
Printed in the United States of America

What's Up Fam,

Can you believe that it's the end of August already? This summer really flew by, but I miss wearing jackets and boots so I'm cool with it.

If you haven't checked out our web series' and movies, make sure that you do. We have quite a few selections for you to get into. Just log onto YouTube and look up T. Styles, her page will come up and all of our productions will be right at your fingers! Enjoy.

Also, we are making ALL of our novels available on Audio Book. So far we have (4) titles available and (2) more completed that will be available within a week. And bonus...T. Styles will be narrating the majority of her own novels! Make sure you get at 'em.

On to the book at hand, "She Brings The Worst Kind". This novel is FULL of drama. I enjoyed reading this from cover to cover in one sitting. That damn Rumor is a mess! I'm sure you will enjoy it too.

With that being said, keeping in line with tradition, we want to give respect to a vet or trailblazer paving the way. In this novel, we would like to recognize:

Kevin Hart

Funny man, Kevin Hart is a stand up comedian who has been telling jokes for years dating back to 2001. However, over the last five years, his star has truly lit up Hollywood. He co-starred in the incredibly funny movie, "Think Like A Man", that was based off the Steve Harvey novel with the same title and he hasn't looked back. Just recently, Kevin added author to his resume' by writing a book called, "I Can't Make This Up: Life Lessons". It's a memoir on success, survival and the importance in believing in yourself. It's a great read and true to anyone who has ever seen a Kevin Hart stand up movie, it will have you laughing out loud! Check it out.

Aight, get to it. I'll catch you in the next novel.

Be Easy!

Charisse "C. Wash" Washington
Vice President
The Cartel Publications

www.thecartelpublications.com

www.facebook.com/publishercwash

Instagram: publishercwash

www.twitter.com/cartelbooks

www.facebook.com/cartelpublications

Follow us on Instagram: Cartelpublications

#CartelPublications

#UrbanFiction

#PrayForCeCe

#KevinHart

CARTEL URBAN CINEMA'S 3rd WEB SERIES

BMORE CHICKS

@ Pink Crystal Inn

NOW AVAILABLE:

Via

YOUTUBE

Don't Want To Wait? Purchase the ENTIRE

Season via DVD Today!

www.youtube.com/user/tstyles74

www.cartelurbancinema.com

www.thecartelpublications.com

CARTEL URBAN CINEMA's 2nd MOVIE

MOTHER MONSTER

The movie based off the book,

"RAUNCHY"

by

T. Styles

Now Available on You Tube

Available to Download via VIMEO

www.cartelurbancinema.com and

www.thecartelpublications.com

CARTEL URBAN CINEMA'S 2nd WEB SERIES

IT'LL COST YOU (Twisted Tales Season One)

NOW AVAILABLE:

YOUTUBE / STREAMING / DVD

www.youtube.com/user/tstyles74

www.cartelurbancinema.com

www.thecartelpublications.com

CARTEL URBAN CINEMA'S 1st WEB SERIES

THE WORST OF US (Season One & Season Two)

NOW AVAILABLE:
YOUTUBE / STREAMING/ DVD

www.youtube.com/user/tstyles74
www.cartelurbancinema.com
www.thecartelpublications.com

CARTEL URBAN CINEMA'S 1st MOVIE

PITBULLS IN A SKIRT – THE MOVIE

www.cartelurbancinema.com and

www.amazon.com

www.thecartelpublications.com

15

#SheBringsTheWorstKind

PROLOGUE

You ever get the feeling that something bad was going to happen even though all you can see in the moment was good? You ever feel like you had enough bad luck and God should go on ahead and leave you be, because you deserve a little happiness for a change?

That was pretty much my life.

Well, sort of.

I had the man I thought I wanted. An apartment I could afford and a job as a customer service rep that paid the bills. Things were going good until *she* showed up.

When I look at my life now I can say people warned me. I can say a lot of things, including that everyone who truly cared about me tried to soften the blow I would be dealt with over the week by six little words.

"Don't let her in your house."

If only I had listened.

CHAPTER ONE

WASHINGTON, DC

JONI

I love these kind of nights.

Bae and me are lying in bed, looking at an episode of *Power*. We saved them up so we can watch them like a movie, snuggle and try to imitate the fuck scenes the show had which were always on point. When Tasha was about to read Ghost for blood again, I laid my head on his chest and he kissed the top of my naturally curly brown hair.

"You got the rent money?" I asked him hoping he'd say yes so we wouldn't get put out.

He sighed. "Things have been real short lately, bae. I have half of it but I'm working out the other half."

I looked at the show. "Well we still going to Atlantic City right?"

He laughed. "How come you keep asking me a million times when you know the answer gonna be yes. Plus we already paid for the room anyway and there's no refund policy this close." He looked down at me. "But you ain't bleeding are you? 'Cause I hate wasting trips when you like that."

I laughed. "When you fucked me was I bleeding?"

He shook his head and we both focused back on the show. "I like Angela but I can't see how he choosing her over his wife," I said.

He sighed. "Be quiet, bae."

"I'm serious." I clutched the pillows.

"So you gonna act like the nigga didn't tell her about his dreams five or six times, only for Tasha to be all about the dope game?" I looked up at him, his neatly cornrowed hair made his light brown eyes pop even more. "After awhile a nigga gonna switch up if his female ain't acting right in—"

His cell phone buzzed again and it was for the fifth time this night. I was trying to hide my annoyance but it was hard. Egan and me had been doing good and I didn't want that to change. After checking his phone he placed it down, kissed the top of my head again and focused back on the show.

Since the screen was placed down, like he always put it, I couldn't tell who had hit him up but I had plans for that later. The moment the show went off and he went to pee, something he always did because I gave his baby bladder ass two bottles of beer, I picked up his phone but the screen was locked.

Fuck.

I used to know his passcode but that changed a long time ago after I texted his mama's friend, thinking she was a female when all the woman wanted was a little help moving to her new house.

When I saw him coming back, I put the phone down and scooted back in place. He lie next to me and started the next episode. "Bae, who was that, that hit your phone earlier? Before you went to the bathroom."

He chuckled.

"Watch the show."

I frowned. "I asked you a question though."

"Why you so insecure?" He asked before grabbing the remote control and placing the show on pause. "If I wanted you to know everything I did on every single day I would tell you. What you need to do is clean this fucking house and maybe I'll start giving you the in's and out's to my business."

My face grew hot with embarrassment and I scratched my cheek.
20

"How you sound?" I sat up. "I cleaned up earlier today."

"So that's why the toilet got brown shit around it and the tub grimy as fuck? 'Cause you cleaning up?"

"Egan, please don't act like—"

"You know what." He got up, slipped into his jeans, grabbed a t-shirt and his car keys. My stomach started ripping because the last thing I liked was to be left alone.

"Where you going?"

He didn't say a word.

"Egan, can I at least go with you?"

He chuckled. "Now why in the fuck would I take you with me when you the one I'm bouncing away from?" He moved toward the door and I followed him.

"Please don't—" he walked out and slammed the door in my face.

The moment he was gone it felt like the walls were tightening up on me. I pulled the covers over my head and tried to tell myself repeatedly that this wasn't real but nothing I did worked. For as long as I could remember I had been afraid of being alone and I was tired of it because I didn't understand my fear.

So with the covers over my head I did something mama always told me to do but I never did.

Pray.

Dear God, please remove this fear from my heart. However you gotta do it I'm okay with it. Just make it go away.

I don't know why but for some reason I was scared the moment the words came out of my mouth. Maybe because mama said it always gets worse before it gets better. I sure hope that ain't true.

JONI

Scared to be alone I called my brother and two things happened that ruined my night. First I got my period and second my brother annoyed me to no end.

I glanced up and looked at my face in the mirror. I can't believe I came on early. Maybe it was my nerves. Egan and me had plans to get out of the house for the weekend and as freaky as we were that always meant hours of sexing and ordering takeout afterwards. Now I was realizing none of that would go down because whenever I got my cycle he would make an excuse on why we couldn't follow through with our plans. And as mad as he was at me right now I knew it would not be different.

It was settled.

I would have to lie.

So, standing in front of the sink in my bathroom, I was washing blood out of my jeans since these were the only clean ones I had left. Everything else was dirty and I had plans to dry these and wear them for tomorrow before begging him to buy me something new to wear later.

"Joni, I hate to tell you this because I'm your brother and all, but that shit's gross." My brother said before yawning because it was two am in the morning.

Looking back at Marco, who now went by Macy because he was trans, I rolled my eyes. "Well if I need your opinion I'll ask for it which ain't happened yet." I paused. "I'm not paying you any attention anyway because you don't even have a man so save your time and breath!" I turned back around and focused on my jeans.

"Oh really? You mad at me 'cause you gross?"

"Macy, just stop."

"Stop what? Egan can't be okay with this shit!" As he sat down on the edge of the tub I saw him squinting his nose from the mirror as he looked around the bathroom. "I mean look at this place, Joni. A bitch's number one priority is to keep a clean house and a clean body." He shook his head. "And you failing like fuck and—"

"Why you still here?" I tossed the jeans in the sink, turned around and folded my arms across my chest. "Because I know it's not to tell me how nasty I am! Besides, you don't stay longer than five minutes when you do come anyway."

"First off you called me because you were scared again." He pointed at me. "But what's the reason I don't stay too long?"

He shook his head and wiped his long braids over the right side of his shoulder. "You know what, I'ma leave all that alone." He took a deep breath. "Anyway, how do you feel about your man's sister coming home?" He smacked his tongue. "Cause if I were you, I would be highly worried and highly concerned."

24

I rolled my eyes.

"On second thought, I would be *highly* concerned and *highly* worried." He giggled like he said something profound.

"I knew it was another reason you were still here."

"Answer the question."

"To be honest I don't feel no type of way."

"Then you're a fool."

I took a deep breath, pulled myself off the sink and stomped toward my room, kicking trash out my path along the way.

"Wait, you're walking away from me while I'm talking?" Macy asked, as he stood right behind me eager to get on my nerves.

"Because I don't wanna do this." I paused. "You acting like my man fucking his own flesh and blood or something." I paused. "And whether she's home or not it doesn't stop the show nowhere over here. Believe that!"

"Ewww...Gross!" He pushed junk off a portion of my bed and flopped down into a small available space. "I never said that they were having sex. But the whole neighborhood knows they really close and people saying that when she's home, and back in the picture, she brings a lot of drama."

"I heard she was nice."

"Well you heard wrong and I'm tired of you being so *'whatever he wants'* about everything. I'm not even just talking about Rumor coming home."

"I hate when you get too deep."

"Girl, if you don't learn to start to give a fuck and to take care of yourself, your life gonna fall out of control." He paused. "Egan not gonna be able to save you from everything."

As I thought about what my brother was saying I remembered when Egan and me first met. My life was pretty much destroyed earlier that day when my boyfriend, the real love of my life, broke up with me early in the morning for no reason. Later that day I was sitting in class, about to take an exam when I was called down to financial aid at UDC because my tuition hadn't been paid in months. All my life I wanted to be a podiatrist even though people laughed when I told them. But my mother who is good with life but bad with finances spent all of the cash my daddy left me when he died in the army.

With no money to pay for college, they threw me out. When I couldn't go back to school I realized all of my dreams of getting out of DC were over. Crying and lost, I walked two blocks down the street trying to figure out what I was going to do with my life when I bumped into Egan. The first thing I remembered when I looked at his face was his light brown eyes.

And then he smiled and he looked even better.

He was wearing a clean white t-shirt and blue jeans and his hair was freshly cut even though his sneaks weren't brand new. "You buying?" He asked me.

I blinked away my tears. "Buying what?"

"Smoke."

"Oh...no...I—" I shook my head rapidly back and forth.

"Why you crying?" He moved closer and put his hand over mine, which was holding my books. "Your dude broke your heart or something?"

"No." I thought about my ex. "I mean kinda but that's not the reason I'm crying. You know what...I really don't wanna talk about this anyway. Besides, I don't even know you."

He looked down at my books. "Oh, you a college girl." He licked his lips. "I like that."

For some reason I got grossed out. Maybe it was because school was over for me but I rolled my eyes and walked away from him when he yanked me so hard my arm got pulled from its socket.

Seriously.

My arm dislocated and since I didn't drive he had to take me to the hospital because I could barely use it. It's definitely what I call a bad first date but had he not grabbed me like he did we wouldn't be together. So there I was, laid up in a hospital bed, looking at the man who was responsible across from me. His T-shirt was dingy and he didn't look as clean as he did earlier because he had to help me off the ground after minutes of screaming and hollering due to the pain I was in.

He walked up to me and stuffed his hands in his pockets. "Sorry, about this shit." He looked at my arm, which was in a cast. "I ain't know I grabbed it that hard."

"What's your name?" I asked him.

He smiled. "Wow, all this and I forgot to tell you my name." Suddenly he frowned. "Wait...you ain't gonna try and sue are you?"

I giggled. "I just wanna know your name."

28

He nodded. "Alright, but I ain't gonna tell you right now."

I frowned. "If not now, when?"

"After I make you fall."

"So you broke my arm and you gonna push me too?"

He walked over to the other side of the bed, dug into my purse, removed my phone and placed his number in the contacts under the letter 'M'. When he was done he put it back. "Your brother gonna be here in a minute right?"

I nodded. "Yep."

"Good, so call me when he gets here. And when you feeling up to it I'll take you out."

For some reason I looked at his shoes again. They looked like they had been worn longer than most dudes I knew. I think he noticed because he said, "Don't judge a book on what you see. It'll be a mistake."

An hour later my brother picked me up and the next morning I texted 'M' because I was interested in finding out a little more about him. He paid for me to catch a cab over his house and I was excited about it all the way over. When I got to his house I was surprised at how nice it was.

The area was suburban and the house looked like some rich folks lived inside.

When I made it to the door everything changed the moment I knocked on it. A bullet flew over my head from inside and I ducked, before three more did the same thing. Confused I turned around to run when I saw five police cars pull up to the house. Seconds later they emptied their cars with guns and moved for the door.

I walked right into the middle of a shoot out and that should've been my queue to leave him alone.

Instead I moved out of their way, just as a really light skin girl, who could pass for white, ran out with a big silver gun in her hand. They kept screaming for her to get on the ground when one officer shot her in the wrist, causing the gun to slam onto the ground. It turned out later that this crazy girl was M's sister and she was arrested by the police, who had been staking out her house all that night.

Although I never got the details on why.

When things calmed down and they were done asking me who I was and where I came from, Egan walked up to me and wrapped his arm around my waist. "I can't believe you stayed here after all of that."

"Me either. Maybe I'm stupid not to have left." I smiled. "So who was that?"

He smiled. "That was my sister and that's all I can say for right now."

"Okayyyyyyy."

"But I have to ask you something else," he said. "So don't be upset but I have to know."

I nodded. "Okay...what is it?"

"How is your credit?" He continued.

"Excuse me?"

"Listen, I'm in a pretty bad situation right now. The government is gonna seize this house and I'm gonna be homeless." He looked back at the bullet-ridden door. "I mean is anything stopping you from making a move with me? Call me crazy but I think we can be good together."

"Other than the fact that I don't know you?"

He nodded. "We could look at it that way or I can ask you another question."

"What's that?"

"What you doing with the rest of your life?"

That was 3 ½ years ago and M who I later found out was called Egan and I, had been together ever since. There was so much I loved about him, like how he fucked me only after playing with my pussy to make sure I was wet. And how he would bring home food most night's cause he knew I didn't know how to cook. And how he didn't mind a junkie house because we were never home anyway.

No matter how great things were with him, he could be critical of me if something didn't go his way too. Or if somebody made him mad he would take it out on me instead. But stuff like that happens in every relationship so I had no real complaints.

I looked over at my brother. "Me and Egan are good Macy so don't worry about us. Plus it's been years since his sister been home so she gonna have to get used to me being in the picture."

"I hope you right about that." He shrugged.

Suddenly I heard a door open and Egan yelled, "Bae, I'm home!"

Macy and me pushed past the trash in the hallway and into the living room where my boyfriend was standing smiling at me. Egan's 6 ft. 1, skinny and ripped up although I don't know how since he never went to the gym. He was holding two paper bags and side of white plastic ones. They stank so good.

"You got my crabs didn't you?" I smiled. "I thought you were mad at me."

"I'm over it."

I smiled harder. "Where did you go this time of night to get 'em?"

"I know a guy." He was still smiling until he looked over my shoulder at my brother. "What I tell you about this faggy being in my house when I'm not here?" He pointed at him.

"Egan!"

He shook his head. "Yo, get the fuck out my house, nigga." He said to him.

Macy placed his hands on his hips and grinned. "No need in you doing all that. I was leaving anyway." He switched toward the door, putting a little extra in his step.

When he was gone Egan said, "Keep him outta my house!" He pointed at me.

"Aight!" I took the bags from him, walked to the kitchen and shoved the trash to the floor to make room for the crabs. I was about to make the sauce when he said, "Oh, and I forgot to tell you that my sister moving in for a little while."

I turned around and crossed my arms over my chest. "Are you asking me or telling me?"

"Cut it out."

"So you found some random crabs in the middle of the night because you want me to let a person who doesn't like me live here?"

"I never said she didn't like you? Where you get that shit from? Stop putting words in my mouth."

"Yes you did!" I moved closer to him. "You said it when you visited that time at—"

"Look, she likes you okay!" He walked away from me and opened the refrigerator. "Stop making a big fucking deal about everything."

"Whatever, Egan."

He grabbed my shoulders softly and looked down at me. "Listen, it will only be for a little while."

"But I don't want somebody else in our house! I'm serious."

"Why? Because of other people?"

"No. I...I mean...I—"

"Do you trust me?"

"Egan..."

He moved my chin so that I had to look dead into his eyes. "Do you trust me?"

"Yes but...I mean...I can't let her live here. I'm sorry. Plus what if whatever she's into this time bites us?"

34

"It won't."

"But what if it does?"

He frowned and backed up. "I'm never gonna forget this, Joni. The day I came to you for help and you denied me."

I looked down. "Well I hope, no, I'm praying that you will. I just gotta stand my ground that's all."

He nodded and walked toward the exit. Before leaving out he turned around and said, "You know...I'ma start needing you to clean up around here too. It's a good thing my sister not moving in after all. You would've embarrassed the fuck out of me with how you keep such a nasty house."

CHAPTER TWO

RUMOR

When I stepped outside of the prison after 3 years I smiled when I saw my friend Jesse waiting to pick me up inside a white Altima. I nodded at her, walked toward the passenger seat and slid inside. When the door closed I looked in the back.

It was empty.

Glancing over at her, she cleared her throat. "Glad you called me to pick you up." She grabbed a few of my fluffy gold curls before letting her hand drop in her lap. "I can't believe how much it's grown. Hair goals for real."

I looked ahead. "Where is he?"

She coughed. "Your brother?"

"I'm not fucking around." I pointed at her. "You know what I'm talking about."

She pulled away and maneuvered into traffic but I could tell she was nervous. "Rumor, stop talking about that again. I told you it ran away."

"And I told you I didn't believe you."

She waved her hand in my face and my body grew hot. The last thing I tolerated was disrespect. "Look you just came home, Rumor. Let's just enjoy the day and if you want I'll buy you another dog."

My pressure rose in my body. I could tell because my fists tightened in my lap and I found it hard to breathe. "You seen Phillip?"

"Nobody has. He's been missing in action since about a year after you were gone."

I nodded. "Take me to your house."

Her eyes widened. "For what? I thought you were going to Egan's at least to visit."

"I got to shower and for now I don't have a place to stay."

"So Egan really not letting you live with him?"

I shook my head. I didn't feel like talking to the lying bitch much anyway. Instead I grabbed her cell phone and called my brother without asking permission. I could feel her little beady eyes on me as she drove down the road. Everything about this girl screamed nervousness. When my call was answered I smiled. "Egan, I'm home!"

"Sis, you have no idea how much I missed your ass!" He paused. In the background I could hear a female laughing and since she was being loud I figured she wanted me to hear her. It was probably his girlfriend Joni. "I miss your little ass. But why you ain't want me to scoop you?"

I turned the volume down on her iPhone so she couldn't hear my conversation since the radio was off and the car was quiet. I knew Jessie's red ass was ear hustling.

"I know but I know your girl doesn't want me staying there. Plus I have a few things to take care of." I glanced over at Jessie who was still looking at me.

"I know my girl ain't feeling it but I'm still working on her. Just give me a few days at the very most." He whispered. "But that don't mean you can get into trouble on your first day out, Rumor! I know your ass."

"Trust me, I won't get into nothing I can't handle." I looked over at Jessie again out the side of my eye. "You can believe that."

"Well let me know when you're done." He paused. "That should give me enough time to settle things on my end. You can still come through for dinner though."

"All I'm gonna say about your girl is this, if you don't have control over her you fell off in my opinion."

RUMOR

When we made it to the apartment building Jesse tapped the steering wheel after parking. I don't know what she was searching for but she was acting weird. After taking a deep breath, out of nowhere she looked around and said, "Dang it! Somebody in my parking space!" She pointed in front of her at a red Honda. "Can you park in that space over there for me?" She pointed at an empty spot. "I'm gonna run upstairs right quick and—"

"Hold up, the red Honda pulling out now." I pointed at the car ahead and the empty space in front of us. "All you gotta do is ease right in."

This bitch tried it.

The last thing she was going to do was walk up stairs into her apartment without me.

After she parked, she slowly walked up the steps and towards her door. I felt like she wanted to tell me I couldn't come in but decided not to.

She put the key in the door, turned around and said, " I haven't been honest." She clutched her hands in front of her. "Milky *is* here."

I grinned and scratched my head. "Open the door, girl. I already knew you had my dog. I just wanted to see how far you would go with your little lie. I'm over it though."

"And you not mad?"

I frowned. "For what? We friends."

She turned around, nodded and dropped the keys before nervously picking them back up. The moment she opened the door an all white Great Dane ran up to me, placing his paws on my shoulders. What was weird was that she stood next to me and after all this time he still chose me to greet. He was a big baby when I got locked up but now he stood on his hind legs, his head over top of mine.

After I happily hugged him, my body smelling like dirty dog now, I walked over to Jesse and wiped her straight black hair behind her ears. "Thanks for taking care of him. He looks really happy and I'm surprised since you live in this apartment."

She nodded. "You...you..."

"No I'm not mad at you."

She wiped tears rolling down her face. "Good, because I'm so sorry. I just fell in love with him and since I don't have a man he was like one to me. Don't think I'm crazy. I just—"

"Jesse! It's cool! Now can you make me something to eat? I'm starved for some real food. As you can imagine it's been three years since—"

"I got you." She said clutching her hands together in front of her. "Leftover spaghetti from last night okay?"

"That's perfect!"

As she warmed up the food I played with Milky. My mind was filled with getting back on top which included getting the money from a job me and some friends pulled off before I got locked up. Somehow the police found out I was involved but none of them got arrested. To this day I didn't know who did me wrong but I had plans on finding that out too.

The dog and me were lying on the floor watching TV when Jesse brought over my plate. I sat on the couch and grabbed it. She was still looking like she was about to shit her thong. "Girl, sit down. Why you hovering over my head?" I grabbed my fork and ate some food. It was pretty good too. "Why you looking all creepy?"

She remained standing.

"Uh...so...what was prison like?" She smiled like a fake mannequin.

"There ain't a lot to tell." I shrugged.

"Well it seems like you changed."

I put my plate in between us. "Is that a bad thing?" I smiled.

"What...no...I...I mean...I'm so used to the violent monster I knew before prison." The moment her butt cheeks hit the couch to finally sit down, I picked up my fork and repeatedly jabbed her in the throat until she was spread out on the floor, the dog lapping at her blood.

Stupid bitch.

Should've never lied to me.

RUMOR

Milky was in the back seat of Jesse's car as I drove down the street. I was looking for someone who meant a lot to me before going into prison and already an hour had passed and I still didn't see him. I can't lie despite the fact that I hadn't heard from him in prison it didn't stop how I felt after all these years. I was definitely still in love.

After talking to this guy I used to buy smoke from, I was finally given some possible good information. When I pulled up on Reisterstown Road in Maryland, at a non-name brand gas station, I saw Phillip sitting on the ground leaning against the frame of the building. His blue jeans were grungy and his shoes were run over. He didn't look nothing like the dope boy that was in my life before I was locked up.

I parked Jesse's car and me and Milky walked up to him, with my dog leading the way. He immediately licked Phillips face and I could tell that although he was drunk, he recognized him too. "Oh my, God! It's the Milkman! How you doing big guy?"

He played with him a little and I smiled and let them have their moment. It wasn't until Philip stood up that he saw me. Now, the smile he was wearing washed away and I could see tears welling up in his eyes. "Damn, Bae." He stuffed his hands into his pockets. "You still beautiful!"

I moved closer. "Phil, it's only been 3 years." I stuffed my hands in my back jean pockets. "But what...what happened to you?"

He frowned and sighed. "How did you find me? In Baltimore?"

"The streets. They always know how to find you, even if you don't want them to."

He shook his head and crossed his arms over his chest. "You always were tapped in to the blocks. Even more than me sometimes." He looked down at his filthy clothes. "Sorry I couldn't get cleaned up for you."

"You're my husband."

"I don't deserve that title anymore."

"How you sound? For better or worse remember?" I stepped closer and Milky stood next to me. "I meant those words when we made our vows. When I was locked up I had two worse fears. Getting locked up again once I was out and losing you."

"But we didn't even have a real wedding. We went to Vegas and—"

"It was real to me, Philip. No matter how short it was."

He looked at me for a moment. "You can't want me like this, Rumor. I ain't got nothing to give you. I'm a zombie for real."

"I want you even more." I said. "You fell a little off when I left but now I'm here to pick you back up. That's what you do when you love someone."

"I'm homeless, Rumor! I don't even have a place to stay!"

"As long as I have a place you can never be homeless! Besides, my brother got a crib we can stay in until we get on our feet."

"I don't know, Rumor. I—"

"Please." I touched his sticky face. Even though it was submerged in dirt, he still looked like he didn't belong out here. Like the streets claimed a diamond and didn't even realize it. Philip was then and will always be a snack. "I'm not leaving here without you." I reached out for him and he finally grabbed my hand.

When we made it to the car he took a deep breath. "I know you got plans but I'm asking you not to do so much that you get in trouble again. You have a temper and—"

"All I wanna do is find Stevie and Lando and get our money." I put my hand on my chest. "That's it, I promise."

He nodded and took a deep breath. "I know where to start. Looking for them I mean."

I smiled. "Good. But do you...I mean...you think they spent it all?"

"No, not with the police watching as hard as they've been. To be honest they been watching all of us. They gave up on me though when they realized how I was living."

"Good." I held his hand. "When we get the paper, and even now to be honest, you got to get clean. I need you to be right in the mind, Phillip! You may have been alone before I came home but you have a family now. Can I count on you?"

"I'm going to give you all I can. That's all I can say."

"But this is not you." I pointed outside. "Laying up alongside gas stations and liquor stores."

"You right." He looked ahead. "I know." He paused. "But you sure you want to kick the Hornet's Nest right now? By looking for the twins? 'Cause I'm telling you I have a bad feeling about this."

"They got our money!" I yelled. "Money I gave up three years of my life for! It belongs to you and me. That don't sound like it's worth fighting for to you?"

He sighed. "I understand."

I started the car. "But you're right about something, with the cops sniffing around we have to clean up some loose ends. Starting with the body I left in this apartment."

His eyebrows rose. "What body?"

"Oh it was nothing," I shrugged. "Just this chick I just killed."

"Damn, Rumor!" He yelled. "Already?"

CHAPTER THREE

JONI

Egan and me had fifteen minutes left before Giant Food Store closed and I realized I forgot milk when we were standing in line. I spent the majority of my time cleaning our apartment earlier since he went on and on about how bad it would look if Rumor saw the apartment like that. Although I didn't agree to her living with us, I did agree to her joining us for dinner.

Two people were in front of us when I said, "I got to go back and get the milk, Egan. I be right back. Hold our space so we—"

He grabbed my arm again, something he enjoyed doing for whatever reason. "Come on, baby." He looked at his watch before looking toward the front of the store and out the window. It was now pouring down raining outside. "She gonna be waiting if she not already there. "

"Egan its just one more thing." I put my hands together. "I promise I'll be quick!" I hurried toward the dairy aisle and picked up some milk and Cheese. When I got back with the milk and other stuff, Egan was texting and had a stank face. Maybe it was because our cart was pushed to the back of the line where six people were now in front of us.

"I'm sorry, Egan. I remembered I wanted to make pancakes in case she stayed the night and—"

"But I told you she was waiting, Joni." He looked down at his phone again. "I mean what the fuck?"

"But I forgot something and—"

"And now it's pouring down harder and shit!" He was being loud and people were watching. "I swear, sometimes I don't even know what I saw in you. You act stupid as fuck if I give you too much time." He walked away. "I'll be waiting out front."

I pushed the cart as I watched him walk toward the front of the store.

"Girl, he was cussing you out when you were gone." A lady with two French braids said. "You better be careful. He's obviously interested in something else the way he was checking his phone."

My stomach turned. The last thing I wanted was us getting into a fight on the day I was officially meeting his sister.

When my food was paid for and bagged, I pushed the cart slowly to the front of the store. But where was Egan?

"Ma'am, the store is closed. You have to leave," a woman said walking behind me.

"Oh...I was just looking for my—"

She pushed the door open. "Ma'am, please we want to leave too. They are calling for thunderstorms and—"

"I got it," I said holding my hand up. "I...I'm leaving." The moment I stepped outside the manager locked the door and I was now stuck holding three bags of food, but where was the car? "Please don't tell me he left me!" I said to myself. As time went by I realized that's exactly what he did.

EGAN

Egan jogged up to a brick building where his partner stood talking to a cute female with two puffballs in her hair. The rain was still pouring down but the awning over their heads protected them from getting wet. With his rent due in a couple of days, he decided to collect from one of the last remaining men who worked for him. "What up, Hash?"

Hash didn't recognize him at first but when he did he said, "What up! I heard Rumor got out the other day. I know it's about to be like old times."

He nodded. "Yeah...but I came about that thing."

Hash looked at the cutie and said, "Can I get up with you later?" She smiled and walked away. "Man, I ain't got your money tonight." He shrugged. "I'm sorry."

"Nigga, you been dodging me for a minute. Ain't nobody fucking around with you."

He threw his hands up. "What can I say?"

When someone beeped a horn Egan turned his head to see where it was coming from. When he turned back he was struck in his face with a gun and knocked to the ground. Hash crawled on top of him and took the remaining money in his pocket, which was Joni's half of the rent. "Sorry, nigga, but it's hard out here." He ran away.

Egan slowly rose to his feet, leaning on the banister for support. Rubbing his bloody head he yelled, "Fuck!"

JONI

I was sitting in a diner a block up from Giant Food Store, which I had to walk to and I was so mad my head hurt. My feet hurt badly and none of the people here would let me use their phones to call Egan. I had no idea what I was going to do.

Two hours later when I looked to the right I saw Egan pull up. I don't know how he found me but he opened the door and stomped in my direction. "Joni, look, my sister gonna have to stay with us. I know you mad but that's all I can tell you right now."

I frowned. "So you leave me in the store and the first thing you say is—"

"Look at my fucking face! I was robbed."

I sat up and leaned in. Now I was worried about him. "When did that happen? When you were at the—"

"It don't matter when it happened." He sat back and rubbed his head. "Look, I know you not feeling this but I gotta put my foot down on this one. If you got a problem with that then maybe we won't be able to work." He grabbed the bags on the table. "Come on. Let's go home."

JONI

When I walked through the door with Egan, Rumor was on her hands and knees scrubbing the kitchen floor. A large white dog lay on my sofa and when Egan locked the door I heard someone flushing the toilet in the back. I grabbed his arm. "You told her to move in already?" I whispered.

"Stop tripping. I told you she was moving in so what difference do it make when I did it?" He pulled away from me. "Aye, Rumor, this my woe,

Joni." Egan walked the groceries into the kitchen before stocking the refrigerator.

Rumor looked at my feet, my legs and then my eyes. When she was done she shook her head. "Whatever."

Trying not to get too upset I took a deep breath. "Hey, Rumor." I waved. "You don't have to do all that. I already cleaned up." I walked toward her.

"If you call this clean I can only imagine what your pussy smells like." She continued to scrub.

"Rumor!" Egan yelled. "Cut that shit out. I told you to be cool."

She stood up, wiped her palms on the yellow towel hanging over her shoulder and extended her hand to me. "You know what, I was wrong for coming at you like that. I'm just disappointed to see my brother pick a girl who don't know how to clean house. Or take care of him right." She shrugged. "But what can I say? You can't help who you love."

I looked at her fingers trying to decide if I should shake her hand or fight her. She already got on my nerves and disrespected me in a major way.

54

"So you going to leave me hanging?" When she said that I decided not to be rude and moved to shake her hand but she yanked it back and said, "You know what, let me not fake it. I don't like you. And you ain't got to be cool with me and I ain't got to be cool with you. Besides, I'm not hitting you off. My brother is."

I looked at Egan hoping he would say something in my defense but he was in the kitchen still putting the groceries up, something he never did.

Just then a cute dude with brown eyes, dressed in Egan's clothes, which included black Adidas and a blue tracksuit, came walking toward us. He stood behind her and Egan walked toward me. "Look, let's stop all of this," Egan said.

"Hold up, Egan I'm almost done," she said. "But let me get a few things clear first. Joni, or whatever your name is, me and mine will be staying with my brother until we get our own place." She removed two hundred dollars from her bra and slapped it in my hand. "But don't worry, we always pay our own way." She looked at the guy. "Come on, Phillip and Milky." She stomped down the hallway. The dog leapt off the sofa and followed her and dude into *our* room.

When the door closed I looked at Egan and pointed at the bedroom door. "Really? That's the kind of person your sister is and you have a nerve to have a problem with me and my brother?" I paused. "I mean what did you say to her about me? There has to be something."

"Come on, man!"

"Egan, I can't with your sister!" I grabbed his hands so he could see I was serious. "You're gonna have to find her another place to stay. Please?"

He took the money out of my palm. "This right here is our rent money. Without her we behind again and gonna get thrown out. Now I know you mad but you gotta get over it."

"But she disrespected me in our own home." I whispered. "Don't even get me talking about that big ass dog leaving hair all over the furniture."

"Joni, shit will be okay! I promise."

I walked away from him and leaned against the wall. "And where are they sleeping again?"

"You heard her." He crossed his arms over his chest. "In our room. But like I said it won't be forever."

56

"Fuck, what does she have on you that you let her treat you like she's doing, Egan? Can't you see I don't like her and she doesn't like me?" What can be—"

He covered my mouth with a kiss that tasted like peppermints and our lips locked. All of a sudden I couldn't remember what got me so messed up in the first place. He lifted me off my feet and didn't put me down until I was face up on the sofa. Next thing I know he removed my jeans and panties and tossed them on the floor.

"Wait...you on your period?" He asked looking at my pad, which was stained lightly with blood.

My legs trembled. The one thing he hated was me being on my period. "A little."

He frowned at first, blew a raspberry and said, "Fuck it. I don't even care."

He pulled the tampon out and his lips pressed against my ear as he slipped into me. Pounding slowly he whispered, "I know shit's fucked up but don't leave me, baby. I love you so fucking much. You know that right?"

My words were trapped in my throat and I felt light. You have to understand, I love this man more than I can explain so hearing that he wanted me as much as I wanted him made me weak.

"You my bitch, Joni. And nothing or nobody will come between us unless we let them."

"Mmmmmmm. I know, baby."

"Tell me who you belong to." He moaned louder.

"You." I scratched his back. "Oh my God I belong to you!"

"And you ain't never leaving me are you?" He pumped harder.

"Never if...if you just...mmmmm." I said when the feeling got too good to finish my sentence.

"You never leaving me." He widened my legs. "Now let me hear you say it!"

"Never, Egan. Nobody can pull us apart."

Egan fucked and sucked my neck for an hour. It felt good but all I kept thinking about was why. He avoided me like the plague during this time of the month and not even ten minutes earlier he hated my guts. So what changed now? I guess we fight but when it comes to our relationship maybe things really are official.

This moment was almost perfect, except for his sister standing in the hallway watching us like a creep.

58

CHAPTER FOUR

RUMOR

Me, Phillip and my brother sat in Jesse's car loading our weapons outside of a laundromat in Washington DC. The person I was waiting for had just pulled her clothes out the dryer and was folding them on one of the tables so we didn't have a lot of time. That bitch inside was one of the people involved in the heist and she had no idea her world was about to change.

"Rumor, you sure this is the best way to go at it?" Egan asked before tucking his gun in his waist, covering it with his black hoody.

"You got another idea?"

Egan wiped his hand down his face and exhaled. He's being so different than he was before I left. Like something was on his mind other than getting money these days. In my opinion pussy made him weak. "Maybe me or Phil can lure her out or something." He paused and looked at the window toward the laundromat. "We just got to get her away from other witnesses. I don't think we need to do anything drastic just yet."

I rolled my eyes because my plan was to run up in there with ski masks and pull that bitch out without a fight. Besides, at the moment she was the only one who knew where the twins were and my half a million dollars.

Let me tell you about my money right quick.

Before I went to prison I got word that Langley, The Laundromat King in DC, was about to go to prison due to tax evasion. Since I fucked him on the side I was aware that after he received the tip on his possible arrest, he stopped putting his money in the bank for fear the government would take it all.

When he found out from the same person that he would be arrested the next day, he decided to take all his cash from his secret locations and dig a hole in the back of his niece's yard. And after what he considered to be his last blowjob from me, he told me where his cash was located during his usual session of bragging.

I grabbed, Egan, Philip, Angela, the twins, Stevie and Lando, who were friends of mine, because The Laundromat King had people sitting on his niece's property, guarding the house although most of them didn't know why.

The worst part of our plan happened when someone made a call to the police, claiming that the money was at me and Phillips' house. Turns out they knew about the stashed money all along and wanted to catch him with it. So they came to my house and arrested me based on the fake tip.

I denied even knowing about the money, which was conveniently missing from his niece's house hours later but the police already had me in their custody. Instead of letting me go, they found out about bad checks I wrote and charged me with that instead. Through conversations in jail I found out that the twins took the money to another location. And to prevent them from spending it, I had a few people I know call the cops daily and put them on their trail. If I couldn't have the money they wouldn't either.

Although the twins were nowhere to be found one of their baby mother's was. And that was Cassandra.

We're talking over $700,000 and I'm not letting nobody take what's mine. I was the one fucking Langley, despite being married, not them so why should they make a come up on me. I never felt guilty about what I was doing because Phillip was always a part of the plan.

"Okay I'll try it but if it don't go my way I'm coming in heavy." I told Egan. "You know me so you know I'm not playing."

"Just give it a chance first, Rumor! I'm trying to keep you out on your first day. Don't fuck everything up if you don't have to!"

I looked over at my husband who was sweating and shivering. "What you think?"

He rubbed his arms and then scratched his hair. "I think I need a drink."

My heart dropped because he was really embarrassing me. I was hoping by me coming back he would *try* and do better but now I wasn't so sure. I placed my hand on the side of his face and said, "Hang in there, Phil. I'm going to help you back on your feet but you got to leave the liquor alone for now. Okay?"

He nodded, rubbed his thighs rapidly and closed his eyes. He was no use to me while going through alcohol withdrawal but when clean nobody was more thorough to me than my nigga. Back in the day he would kill at will, take what was his and let the public sort it out. But now things were different.

I looked back at Egan and sighed. "Okay, bring her to me. I'll be out here waiting. For as long as I can anyway."

EGAN

Egan walked into the laundromat and up to Cassandra who was folding clothes while listening to music in her headphones. Two long French braids ran down her back and her pretty face had a sheet of sweat due to it being so hot. The way Egan saw it was he had two options. Number one, he could snatch her out with the world watching or number two, he could use his charm.

He chose the latter.

Smoothly, he walked closer to her. "Now why would somebody as fine as you be here folding clothes alone?"

She took her headphones off. "Excuse me?"

"You heard me. Your man crazy or something? To let you be out here by yourself?"

She rolled her eyes and put the headphones back on, although the music was off. "Get away from me."

"Wow. So busy you can't even hold conversation with a nigga?"

She sighed deeply. "I'ma be straight up with you. I don't need new friends. All I wanna do is fold my clothes and...hold up...why you look familiar?"

When he came inside he forgot that he was involved with the plan to get the money from Langley. The good part was that she wasn't so he was hoping he could get around it. "A lot of people think they recognize me but be wrong." He looked her over. "But look, I just came over here because I just finished with my clothes and was about to get nice." He paused. "You smoke?"

Her eyes lit up. He had her now. "Yeah. Why you asking?"

"Got smoke outside if you interested." He pointed at the door with his thumb. "I'm gonna be honest, that's my real reason for approaching you."

She grinned. "Why you ain't say something before? I could always use some—"

Rumor bolted into the laundromat wearing a ski mask, totally off plan. "Everybody on the fucking floor!"

Everyone but Egan dropped where they were, afraid of getting shot. Quickly Rumor moved up to him and handed him one of the guns. "I got it from here, Egan!"

"What you doing?!" He asked through clenched teeth. He was livid at everything but especially her saying his name. "I fucking had it, man!"

"I was tired of waiting. Besides, I already been waiting for years." Rumor grabbed Cassandra by the arm and violently escorted her outside. "I'm getting my money fuck you think I'm doing?"

When she was outside, Philip jumped out of the car just as they exited the laundromat. When Rumor shoved her against the car, Phillip pushed her inside before sliding next to her. Rumor rushed to the driver seat while Egan slid in the passenger side.

Rumor yanked her mask off and Cassandra finally saw her face. "Oh, my God, Rumor! Why are you doing this?"

Rumor turned around. "Shut up, bitch!"

"Please don't do this to me! I don't know nothing about your money, Rumor I swear to God. You're doing this for nothing. I—"

Phillip stole her in the face, knocking her out cold. Rumor smiled at him while Egan shifted anxiously in the seat. It was only day one and already she brought the drama with her. Everything happened so quickly and he was positive that they drew a lot of witnesses. He was so angry he could hardly sit still and yet he knew she was just getting started.

CHAPTER FIVE

JONI

After my mother made a huge meal for me and my brother, which meant one thing, she wanted to talk about something, I was trying to find a good lie on how to leave. But since I was the guest of honor I knew it wasn't going down.

"So how is Egan?" She sat a bowl of cheese and sour cream mashed potatoes on the table, before sitting down. "Are you two still going good? Because your skin looks healthy. Like you living right."

"You mean what's good with Egan other than him being a homophobic ass?" Macy asked chomping on the chicken.

My mother slapped him so hard his head spun. "Language!"

"Okay, Mama!" He said rubbing his head. "Damn!"

"Don't okay Mama me!" She pointed at him right before farting. Mama farted all the time but never broke conversation to say excuse me. It was just her way. "Anyway if that man don't like you stay outta his house. Speaking of house..." She turned toward me. "I hear Rumor is home. And that they never found that money she stole either. And that means one thing, trouble for you and yours."

I shrugged. "Mama, I don't know nothing 'bout her or no money."

"So why she staying in your house?"

I turned toward Macy. "Really? You ran and told Mama that quick? I just told you the other day!"

He sat back in his chair and crossed his arms over his chest. "What? She asked if Rumor was moving in and I told her yes. What you want me to do? Lie to our own—"

"Shut up, big mouth!" I pointed at him. "I'm never telling you nothing else."

"Don't be mad at your brother. Besides, the whole neighborhood knows she staying with you and shouldn't be. You can look in her eyes and tell she trouble. And I'ma say something else to you too." She pointed at me. "The longer she stays the more damage she'll do to your relationship."

"Mama, I can't tell Egan not to let his sister stay with us." I threw my hands up in the air. "It's his house too remember? You always said that the main reason girls can't keep men is 'cause they don't let them run the house."

"Yeah, I was dumb when I told you that too. And when I did say it was referring to the right man. A good one. 'Cause no man should force another woman on his woman if she not comfortable with it. And that goes for the women in their bloodline too."

"That's not fair, mama."

"Listen, Joni." She scooted closer to me in the chair, scratching the hardwood floors in the process. "You need to do all you can to get that woman outta your house before she destroys your life like she did her own."

"Mama!"

"I'm serious, Joni! Get her out of your house now because that woman brings the worst kind."

"The worst kind of what?"

"The worst kind of everything!"

JONI

I left my mother's house completely annoyed. I was so irritated that on my way to the car I dropped my keys and was immediately stole in my face with a closed fist by a stranger. I hit the ground and when I rolled over and saw two men staring down at me with their faces covered in masks. I knew I was about to die when I saw one was carrying a knife. Just that quickly my life flashed before my eyes.

"Please don't hurt me!" I begged. "I don't have any money."

"Then tell your man and that bitch to back off!" One of them said with a grumpy voice.

Tears roll down my cheek. "Who...what are you talking about?" I cried, the cool ground under my body.

"You heard me! Tell him to back off or I'm a find you again and finish you off." They both ran away.

JONI

When I stormed into my apartment I was surprised that nobody was home. I needed my boyfriend and not only was he not answering the phone but he wasn't there for me. What if something happened and they killed me? It hadn't even been forty-eight hours and already my life was spiraling out of control with Rumor in the mix.

I rushed toward the refrigerator and removed a frozen steak for my eye while wondering who those men were. Even if they were beefing with Egan and Rumor what did I have to do with it? And who was I to tell Egan to stay away from her?

Walking out of the kitchen I stopped short when the massive dog started growling at me. It must have smelled the meat and I was sure it was about to lunge when the door opened and Rumor, Egan and Phillip walked inside.

"Hey, doggie!" Rumor said when he ran up to her and licked her in the mouth. "Did you miss me already?"

Egan walked toward me, with wild eyes looking over my bruised face. "Bae, what happened to you? Got into a fight or something?"

I grabbed his hand and took him toward our room.

"Don't be in there too long!" Rumor yelled. "I wanna get ready for bed. Besides, we had a long night." She paused. "Didn't we, Egan?"

Egan shook his head and sighed.

"What is she talking about?" I asked him.

"Don't worry about it."

I rolled my eyes and pulled him into the room before closing the door. "Who is after you, Egan?" I whispered.

"I don't know what you talking about." He touched my cheek. "But what happened to your face?" He asked seriously.

"A man hit me and he had somebody else with him." I said angrily. "They told me to tell you and that bitch to back off." I grabbed both of his hands. "Egan, what's going on? I never had to worry about being hurt before she moved here and now I'm uncomfortable. In my own neighborhood!"

He walked away and flopped on the edge of the bed. "Fuck, shit is getting out of control

73

already." He threw his hand in his face. "That's all I can say for now." He looked up at me. "I'm not saying I know who those dudes were but I have some ideas."

"Have some ideas?" I walked closer to him. "Are you serious? What if they would've killed me?" I sat next to him. "Do you even care about this? You seem too easy going about it."

"Joni, I wish I could give you more but that's all I can say for now." He put his hand on my thigh. "Plus I don't want you involved with everything I got going on."

"How come before your sister came home you were all regular? And now you gangsta, with people hunting you down and me too?" I walked away from him and he followed. "Egan, I really don't think it's going to work with Rumor here."

He looked down at me.

"Egan! Say something to—"

BANG! BANG! BANG!

"Egan, I know you not in there telling my business." Rumor yelled from the other side of the door.

He grabbed both of my hands. "Work with me for a few days," he whispered. "I will pull us out of this but you have to be careful out here until shit clear up, Joni. To be honest I prefer if you just stay in the house because at least I know you're safe."

"Egan, I have a life? And I already feel like an invader in my own home!"

"Just do that for me? Please! That's all I can say to you right now. Okay?"

I snatched away from him. "Whatever, Egan."

He kissed me and opened the door where Rumor was on the other side, grilling me as usual.

CHAPTER SIX

RUMOR

I walked into the motel where my friend Dolly was watching Cassandra, the girl I pulled out of the laundromat. She was tied up on a chair, looking at me like she didn't know what was going on. Like she didn't know where my money was which was a fucking lie.

I focused on Dolly. Her jeans were soiled and her hair was thrown in a sloppy bun on top of her head. It looked like she was falling off and I wondered why it seemed like everybody's life had cracked up when I was locked up.

"Bitch, what took you so long?" Dolly asked with her hands on her hips. "Got me in here with this hoe you got gagged and tied." She pointed at her. "I ain't sign up for this shit."

I tossed my purse on the bed. "Why you acting like you didn't know what I wanted from you when I called?"

"You said...I mean..." She screamed. "Look, I told you I had to go to work when you said you needed a favor. Had I known I would be committing a crime I would have never came. My kids—"

"Don't even fuck with you so don't pretend to be the greatest mother on earth."

"This is an extreme waste of my time, Rumor."

I reached in my pocket and dangled a bag of crack. "You sure about that?"

Her eyes lit up and she rushed to her purse on the bed looking like she just hit the lottery. It's amazing how she was about to give me the business but now none of that mattered. She was always a sucker for crack and I guess that would never change. My only problem was back in the day she used to keep herself up but now...well...it doesn't matter. She grabbed the sack from me and disappeared into the bathroom.

I walked up to Cassandra and sat on the edge of the bed across from her. I removed the gag from her mouth. "Please, don't do this, Rumor. I'm thirsty! Can you give me some—"

I hit her in the mouth and watched blood pour from her lips. "I'm not here to wait on you so there ain't no need in you begging. That shit won't work over here."

"What happened to you?" She asked. "You always been kind of evil but you're worse now.

Was it prison? Because I never seen this much hate in your eyes before today. This, what you're doing to me, is going to come back on you in the bad way."

"My Money."

"And I said I don't have your money. I live in the same place I did before you went to prison and—"

I hit her again. "I got all day, Cassandra. Do you?" I scooted closer. "Can you really take more of this pain? Because I can deliver if you think you can handle it."

She looked down and took a deep breath. "I don't have your money but...I heard the twins moved it." She shrugged. "As far as I know they hid it somewhere."

"Where?"

"I don't know, Rumor. I think Virginia or something."

I smiled. "What part?"

"Rumor, are you gonna kill me?"

"I just want my money." I paused. "That's it. I did 3 years for a crime I didn't get paid for. Y'all niggas got away free but not me. So knowing all of this how far do you think I'll take it?"

"Alexandria, Virginia." She took a deep breath. "You act like I was a part of that. To be honest I don't think you have to go looking for them." She swallowed. "I heard they already looking for you."

I frowned. "How you figure?"

"They know you home, Rumor. Everybody does. And when I was at the laundromat one of them called to ask if I seen you. So if you really want to find them, to be honest, all you gotta do is wait."

I looked around the room. "Your phone. Where is it?"

"In my purse."

I got up, grabbed her cell and said, "Which number?"

"The last one that called me." I walked over to her. "But what you about to do?"

"When I call, tell him to meet you at your house later. But if I get any idea that you're being sneaky I'm gonna kill you."

She nodded and I dialed. When someone picked up I could hear him say, "Where you at? My aunt been asking 'bout you. Said something 'bout you should've been home a long time ago. You okay?"

She cleared her throat. "Yeah, uh, I just made a stop after washing clothes, Lando. Where my hubby?"

"He in the house. So where you now?"

"Home." She looked at me. "I'm about to cook some mac and cheese and fried chicken with greens. You wanna grab some? You never could refuse my food so you might as well say yes."

"Yeah, I got you." He chuckled. "See you in a minute. And be careful. Rumor out here and I don't know what that crazy bitch gonna do."

She looked at me. "I will."

When the call ended I tossed her phone on the bed. "Good job."

"You gonna let me go now?"

"Not until I see them and get my money." I put the gag back on her mouth. "And don't ask me again."

RUMOR

"Look, he's going to be there later so we have to go now," I said to Egan in the living room. "All you gotta do is be on the lookout in the hallway while I go inside the apartment." I looked at my husband. "And don't worry, he's going with us. To watch our backs outside."

"No offense, but your man a drunk. He can't do nothing for me."

I frowned before turning around and looking at Phillip. He was still at his worst, which was embarrassing, but at the end of the day he was still my husband.

"Listen, Rumor, this nigga not solid and if I was you I wouldn't put your life in his hands." He moved closer. Now I'm doing this for you but you're moving too fast. Making a whole lot of decisions that's breaking up on other niggas. You gotta slow your roll."

I sighed. "Are you going with me or not?"

He looked around just as his nasty girlfriend walked out of the bedroom. I swear Egan been slow and soft ever since he got with her. "Yeah, I'ma roll." He wiped his hand down his face.

"Good, let's bounce. We're already wasting too much time."

The three of us were walking to the door when that bitch grabbed Egan's hand. "Don't go. Please. I'm still scared about what happened and I don't wanna be left alone."

"You know what...I can't do this right now." He pulled away from her and followed me toward the door.

Right before we walked out, I winked at her.

CHAPTER SEVEN

JONI

Ever since Egan left my nerves have been wrecked. I thought I heard somebody knock on the door but when I opened it nobody was there. I was too nervous that whoever hit me was going to do it again. I needed to be around someone who I felt could protect me.

So I ran all the way to the building over from mine to find my friend Cheese. Egan took my car so I didn't have a ride there. Cheese and me had our problems but the one thing I loved about him was that he never backed down from trouble.

When I knocked on his door a nine-year-old boy with soggy Avengers underwear, opened it wide. I could still see the pee running down his leg. Fucking gross! "Uh...Is Cheese or Roland here?" I looked inside from where I stood.

He slammed the door in my face.

"Okayyyyyyyyyy." I was headed down the stairs when I heard loud music outside of the building. I jogged toward the exit and pushed the door open. When I saw a navy blue Charger I smiled before rushing toward it quickly.

Cheese and Roland were inside rolling a blunt and I thought about how I could've been someone else meant to do them harm. Standing near his driver side I knocked on the window. Startled, Cheese reached for something under the seat and I sighed relieved.

"It's just me!" I said raising my hands.

"Oh shit!" Cheese said before rolling the window down and lighting a blunt. "You finally left your man and realize I'm where it's at?"

I smiled but then grew serious. "Nah, I'm here on some other things. I need some protection I guess."

"You gonna ride this dick first?" Cheese pumped several times and Roland busted out laughing.

"I'm serious!"

"And so am I!" He winked and I forgot how cute he was. He wore a low-cut and his gold chain hung over the white wifebeater.

I put my hands on my hips. "Are you gonna help me or not?" I asked.

"Not." Cheese said.

I rolled my eyes and walked away. I could hear the door open and Cheese rush up to me. "I'm just playing." He grabbed my hand, something
84

that always made me nervous. "You used to be fun." He walked me back toward the car.

"I hate when you around Roland because you treat me so different."

"I'm sorry," he said honestly.

"Look, I'm having a lot of trouble now, Cheese. I really need your help."

He nodded and opened the back car door. "Get inside."

I eased inside and for some reason put my seatbelt on. I guess it was because Cheese was a horrible driver so I wanted to be prepared in the event he pulled off without letting me know.

"So what you need?" Cheese asked.

"First off some kid answered the door in dirty undies in your apartment, Cheese. He in there by his self?"

They both laughed.

"Nah, my crack-hoe-gritty-teeth-stank-pussy-broke-baby-mama in there," Roland interjected. "Did I say she was trifling too?"

"Yeah." I frowned. "I think you cleared that up enough."

"But what you need?" Cheese asked.

"Somebody threatening me."

They looked at each other.

"What the fuck for?" Roland asked. "You ain't in the streets."

"Rumor's home." I said. "And she staying with me. I'm not sure but I think it got something to do with that."

Cheese sighed. "Oh yeah, I heard about that. And if I didn't fuck with you I'd put you out my ride. That bitch is exclusive trouble and with the things I got going on right now I can't be involved." He turned around and looked into my eyes. "Not even for you."

"Yeah, I know."

"Do you really?" Roland asked. "Only people she touches gets mixed in to her drama and right now we're out of it."

I sat up. "Please help me! Some dudes laid me down on the ground earlier tonight when I was leaving my momma's house. And I think she may be involved."

"And you thought that would help your case why?" Roland asked. "If anything we should be further away from you."

"Because—"

"What do you want from us?" Cheese asked. "And where your man at? The last I heard from

86

you he was the second coming, and now you asking me for help? This ain't adding up, Joni."

"I know but I'll pay you."

"You got money?" Roland asked with raised eyebrows. "Enough to hire us and convince us to get involved in this shit? I heard about that paper that Rumor looking for too, so I know you can lay hands on it if you applied yourself."

"If she got money she ain't giving none to me. She don't even like me."

"Well that ain't our problem right, Cheese?" Roland asked, tapping him on the arm. "Sounds like we too expensive for you."

Cheese cleared his throat. "Basically."

I thought about my job. I could probably get some money from my 401k but I'm not sure how much because I squeezed it a lot.

"Get out the car, man." Roland said to me.

I looked at Cheese. "Please don't do this. I—"

Suddenly we were under attack by gunfire. The first bullet knocked the weed out of Cheese's hand. The second one went through the window and hit the stop sign. We all ducked and Cheese hit the gas so hard we almost spun out. I don't even know how he turned the car back on that quickly. "Who were those niggas?" Cheese yelled as he continued to speed down the street.

I looked behind us and back at him. Everything was so confusing.

"Was them the niggas who were after you or not?" Roland asked.

"I don't know." I turned back around to face them. "Maybe."

Roland looked at Cheese. "Them niggas just shot at us, bruh. Guess we're involve now after all."

JONI

When we went back to Cheese's house, the little boy had the same pissy underwear on he did when I first knocked on the door about an hour earlier. The only difference now was that his underwear was dried and he stank. Which is why I don't understand why he chose to sit in my lap.

After getting shot at I tried to reach Egan and each time I was unsuccessful. And since I didn't know who shot at us in front of the building I wasn't going home until he was there. I had the cell phone against my ear. "Egan, I don't know where you are but please call me. I need your help."

CHAPTER EIGHT

RUMOR

After all this time I'm finally ready.

Nothing is gonna stop me from getting my money. So I'm standing inside Cassandra's bedroom and all the lights are turned off. I'm waiting for Stevie or his twin brother Lando to come inside. My .45 was tucked in my waist and ready to fire if he acted like he didn't wanna give me the information on where my money was located.

My plan was simple. The moment Philip, who was parked outside in a stolen truck, texted me and said they were there, I would unlock the door for them to come inside. If they didn't twist the knob on their own I would send a text from Cassandra's phone to come inside.

Egan was also on the job and would be waiting in the hallway upstairs ready to follow Stevie or Lando into Cassandra's crib. Of course Egan wanted no part of my plan originally but he came around when he realized the streets didn't fuck with him after he let somebody rob him and get away with it. He needed this money as much as I did.

PHILLIP

Philip sat in the car as his body was going through severe withdrawals. Despite sitting down every limb was uncomfortable as he waited for it all to be over. Looking out the window he said, "Man, where are you niggas?" He said to himself. "Cause I ain't got a good feeling about this."

Although cars rolled up and down the street he grew anxious when he saw two men walking on the curb across from where he was parked. The pedestrians eventually plopped on the steps in front of a brownstone as they talked loudly while drinking liquor covered in a brown paper bag.

The moment he saw the exchange he salivated, licking his lips and then wiping them rapidly. "If only I could have a sip shit would be so much better."

RUMOR

I heard the door open in the front room and my heart dropped. Why didn't Phillip tell me they pulled up? He knew what kind of car they had because Cassandra told us so I could relay the information to him. I was about to call Egan to warn him that I was possibly about to be ambushed when I heard heavy whispering that didn't sound like Stevie or Landon.

I looked around Cassandra's bedroom for a way out. The window was across from me and I decided to try my hand when the door opened. Afraid, I dropped to my knees and crawled under the bed. Once the light was turned on I could see two sets of feet moving around. "Cassandra, you here?" A male voice asked.

"We shouldn't be in here, man." Another male voice responded. "We ain't got a warrant."

"Who cares? She's the one who wanted to meet us at her house." He paused. "That means we can do whatever we want."

"Not exactly." The second man replied. "Now I follow you everywhere but this doesn't feel right. We have to find some other way to nail Rumor and this isn't it."

There was a long build of silence and I hoped he took his partner's advice to leave, otherwise I would be trapped. As I heard them talking I thought about the obvious, that Cassandra was working with the police to find the money they thought I had in my possession. My only question was if they were doing their jobs or just trying to take the money for themselves?

"Okay, call Cassandra back and find out why she's not answering her phone. She can play games if she wants but I highly suggest that she don't."

"Okay but let's get out of here!"

I didn't breathe until I heard them close the bedroom door followed by the front door. I now know the real reason I got out early from prison. It was so I could lead them to the money. But what I didn't know was that Cassandra was working with the police. Had I not snatched her when I did, I could have gotten thrown back into prison just for questioning her about the money.

Nah.

I can't have that.

It was time to think of another plan no matter who got hurt.

CHAPTER NINE

JONI

I have been trying to reach Egan for hours and still nothing. My head was throbbing and I was trying not to cry but I was worried about him and myself. Who was I if he wasn't in my life.

"You want to hit this?" Cheese asked as he drove down the street using his knee. His hands used for passing and smoking the blunt. "I figured you'd want your mind to be a little calm right now."

I put my phone in the seat next to me and looked out the window. "Nah, I'm good."

He sighed. "Look, you can't be tripping over that bop." Cheese said. "If he feeling you he'll reach out but stop blowing up his phone like you some side broad. You not even hitting my phone and you're getting on my nerves. Sit back and relax and let him come to you."

I rolled my eyes. He didn't understand. "Where we going?"

Cheese passed the blunt to Roland. "Nowhere big." Cheese said. "I got to meet a few folks, collect a few bucks and say a few things. Don't

95

worry, you won't be in the way. Just sit back and keep your lips sealed."

"How long you think that'll take?"

"Do it matter?" Roland asked blowing clouds in the air. "You wanted help and that means you stuck with us for the rest of the night. Unless you want us to drop you off at your crib."

"No." I cleared my throat. "Please don't."

"Now do you want to hit this or nah?" Cheese asked again.

I took it but after coughing hard I gave it back just as he parked the car in front of a strange brick building. We got out and walked up some steps where there were doors the color of blood. For some reason I felt like I was floating and I realized the weed was responsible. When we finally stopped Cheese knocked on the door and a toothless woman wearing a blue Mumu opened it. She seemed happy to see him.

"Cheese, come on in, baby!" She stepped back and we walked inside. "We were expecting you. I see you still looking good."

"Where Joe?" Roland asked standing next to the door while me and Cheese sat on two wooden chairs in the living room. There was no sofa. "He said he was here. We not waiting around here all day."

"He in the back." She scratched her face, which had so many craters on it; it looked like the surface of the moon. "But you got something extra on you? Just a little piece to get me right until I get my check tomorrow? I swear I'ma pay you. Plus you know I'm good for it."

"Fuck outta here!" Cheese waved the air. "Now go get your man. I'm growing impatient."

The woman rolled her eyes and walked into the back. I heard loud sirens outside that seemed to be coming from everywhere and getting closer. Curious, Roland and me walked over to the window and pushed the curtains to the side. Outside people were coming out of their apartments and flooding the courtyard while six police cars drove on the ground quickly leaving dust clouds.

"We came at the right time, Cheese," Roland said. "Cops spread all out this bitch."

Just then officers exited their vehicles with guns aimed at two men who were fighting in the middle of a growing crowd. Suddenly one officer shot up in the air stopping the fight. Having seen enough, I backed up from the window and tripped over the glass table because so much was going on and I was still high. Cheese helped me to my seat just as a really tall and fat man came from the back. He was holding crumbled bills and the white soiled t-shirt he wore made him look extra stinky. The woman was behind him, still smiling widely.

"We're going to have to stay a little while." Roland said to Cheese. "It's too hot out there right now."

"This starting to be a fucked up night!" Cheese took the money and stuffed it into his pocket after counting it to be sure it was right.

"Can I get it now?" The man asked.

"Nah," Roland interjected. "We gonna leave in a second."

"But you got my money."

Cheese looked at Roland. "I don't think you should give it to him, Cheese," Roland said. "You remember what happened last time."

"Man, I'm not gonna hit it. Please!"

Cheese looked at the man. "I'ma give this to you now but do not hit this shit while we in here. Am I clear?"

"Of course, Cheese. I wouldn't disrespect you like that."

98

Cheese handed him the drugs and he turned to walk away.

"Hey, where you going?"

"The bathroom," the man said.

"I'm serious, no smoking in here." He pointed at him. "You gotta wait until we bounce first."

When he left, Cheese walked up to me. "You good? That weed looks like it got you bent."

I nodded rapidly and pulled my phone from my pocket to call Egan. He snatched it away. "Why you do that?"

"Because the nigga not 'bout you right now so stop pushing it." He paused and gave it back. "How many times do I gotta tell you? Stop acting like a bird before I slap the fuck outta you."

Roland looked out the window. "Fuck, when are they leaving?" He shook his head and then looked over Cheese's shoulder. "Aw, man. Cheese, look at this nigga." Roland said pointing.

Cheese turned around and the man he gave drugs too was on the floor in the hallway naked. His limbs moved around like they weren't connected to his body or he was possessed by something that had a strong hold on his mind.

"Fuck!" Cheese said as he placed hands on the side of his face. "I thought I told this nigga not to smoke that shit in front of us!" He said to Roland before looking back at him.

The way his body ticked and cracked his movements reminded me of the movie *The Grudge*. "Oh my goodness," I said holding my hand over my mouth. "What's he on?" I asked Roland, before hiding behind him.

"Flakka."

I didn't know much about drugs and their side effects, but I knew enough about flakka to know it was one of the worst ones for people to be on. I once saw a man on the street bite into his own arm and it scared me as much then as it does now. "I wanna get out of here." I said. "Can't we just leave? The cops not gonna bother us are they?"

"I wanna bounce too but now is not the time." Roland said. "We—" All of a sudden Roland's eyes widened. "Aye, nigga! What you doing?"

He was talking to the man who jumped on Cheese for what look like no reason. His mouth was open and he was trying to bite Cheese's face. Luckily Cheese kept a firm grip of his throat by pressing on it with his forearm. Roland ran to help Cheese by laying hands on the man when all of a sudden the addict took his attention off
100

Cheese and put it on him, eventually knocking Roland to the floor. With Roland out the way the addict turned on Cheese again and grabbed the gun that was tucked in the back of Cheese's jeans.

Roland must've saw this because he ran toward him and was shot in the center of the chest.

Time seemed to stop and I had never seen anything like this before.

Cheese's eyes widened as he ran toward his brother who had blood oozing out of his body.

"Oh my God! Don't do this!" Cheese lifted his brother's head. "Don't die on me, man. Please."

When I looked toward the addict he was crawling on the floor and tweaking like he had no idea that he just committed murder. Or did he? He was so crazy he took to biting the woman who was now screaming at the top of her lungs on the top of her foot. Cheese suddenly got up, took the gun that was now sitting on the floor and shot him in the back of the head.

I threw up where I stood.

JONI

Me, Cheese and the woman were sitting on the chairs looking out into the living room. Cheese's eyes were bloodshot red and every so often tears rolled down his face and he'd wipe it away roughly.

The two bodies lay on the floor in front of us.

Cheese looked at me. "Check again."

I got up and looked out the window. "Yeah. They all gone now." I sat back next to him. "We leaving? Because I can't...I can't stay here a moment longer. My...my stomach hurts."

He nodded and looked at his brother and the addict. Focusing on the woman he said, "Repeat what I told you. I need to make sure you got it right."

She had been crying so she sniffled a little. "I'm 'spose to tell the cops that my man shot Roland."

"And what else?"

"To wait until you've been gone for fifteen minutes before I call." She clasped her hands in front of her. "That's good right?"

He nodded. "If I find out you said anything else I'm gonna come back for you. You know that right? 'Cause everything in my heart telling me to be done with you once and for all. But I'm trying to leave you alive."

"I understand." She nodded. "But who do I say shot my man?"

"Who you think?" He paused. "Why you think I'm leaving the gun?"

"But they won't believe I shot him in self defense."

Cheese grinded his teeth and I could tell all patience was lost a long time ago after his brother was killed. Taking a deep breath he reached into his pocket and pulled out a sack before tossing it in her lap. "Do you think you can convince them now?"

She smiled. "Yep, it was definitely self-defense."

"He shot my brother and you shot him when he dropped the gun. He's on that flakka so they definitely will believe you killed him. If nothing else because you was afraid he'd kill you next. He

103

already bit into your foot. Show 'em," He pointed to her wounded foot. "And that's all you gotta say." He stood up and looked down at her as she tore into the drugs. "Dirty bitch." He looked at me. "Let's go."

CHAPTER TEN
RUMOR

I have been in Cassandra's neighborhood for hours because when I came outside Philip wasn't in the car and I didn't see Egan either. Before I went looking for him I needed to find my husband first. So when I finally saw four men in a huddle on the side of the house I walked toward them.

"Hey sexy." Bum One said.

I moved closer to them. "I'm looking for somebody."

"I can be that somebody for you." Bum One continued, showing his toothless smile. "Besides, I like what I see."

They all laughed.

I rolled my eyes. "I'm looking for someone else."

"I understand all that but I'm trying to see—"

"Wait!" Bum Two said covering his mouth, interrupting his friend. "Are you talking about brown eyes? About six feet something tall?"

I swallow the lump in my throat. "Yeah his eyes are brown. So what?"

They all laughed hard again.

"Fuck is so funny?" I asked.

"We seen him alright," Bum One said. "And he's in apartment number 7 down the block. You'll see him too if you go looking. But don't say we didn't warn you."

Something was up. By the looks on their faces it was obvious that everyone was in on the joke but me. "Will the person... living there or whatever, let me in?"

"Sweetheart, the door to the apartment is always open. Trust me." Bum One said. Before they all broke out into laughter again.

RUMOR

I ran all the way to the building they told me to enter. I knocked a few times on the door but when no one answered I twisted the gold knob and walked inside. What I saw made me sick to my stomach. Philip was on his knees sucking another man's dick. "Oh my God!" I screamed. "What are you doing?"

He jumped up and wiped his mouth. "Rumor, uh...what you doing in here? I mean...how did you know I would be here?"

I ignored him and looked around the dump for his jeans, which were also off, but I couldn't find them anywhere. The apartment had trash throughout and it looked and smelled like a dope house. When I finally found his pants I said, "Put these on and lets go. I wanna leave out of here immediately!"

"But he wasn't finished!" The man fucking my husband said.

I pointed at him. "The way I feel right now the last thing you wanna do is fuck with me."

"But I gave him crack!" He yelled. "And he smoked it so now he owes me."

I stumbled backwards upon hearing the news. I knew he was an alcoholic but my heart broke even more over finding out that he was a drug addict too. I had no idea he had fallen this far and now I wished I could forget.

RUMOR

Philip sat in a tub of warm water inside a motel room I rented. I was washing his back softly trying to understand what was happening to him and our relationship. I knew I was gone for three years but he fell like ten years had passed between us. I decided to come to a motel because I wasn't sure if the cops were waiting on me at Egan's place and I needed some time to think alone with him.

"That feels nice." He said as I squeezed warm water on his back with the rag.

"I'm glad," I said softly.

He looked into my eyes. "Why you still love me?" He asked. "After what you saw tonight?"

"You can't be serious."

He stared at me with sad eyes. "I need to know why you love me so hard, Rumor. You know I don't deserve it."

I exhaled. "Phillip, do you remember when you told my mother you wanted to be with me?" I paused. "Because they tried to make us stay apart from each other? Saying we shouldn't be together and all that?"

He laughed. "How could I forget?"

"My mother said, *"You look like a good man. A handsome one at that. Why would you want to date my daughter who had all five of her kids taken away from her by the Department of Social Services, a record longer than the trip from here to Texas and a nasty attitude?"*"

He chuckled. "I didn't pay your mother any mind." He paused. "She was—"

"Right. My mother was right about me. But you stayed by my side anyway, even helped me get on my feet. And if I didn't trust the wrong people you would not have been forced to testify against me in court about the bad checks. All I wanna do now is what's right by you. I know you started using drugs out of guilt and I'm telling you it's okay."

"I should have never let them convince me to betray you, Rumor. Just to save myself. But I have to be honest, I was on drugs even when we were married."

My eyes widened. "No you weren't."

"I was, Rumor. Listen to the truth when someone is giving it to you. I don't deserve you. If you wanna live and be happy you have to let me go. Look at where you found me tonight? All I'll do in your life is make matters worse. I'm not the man you knew before you got locked up and after tonight I think it should be clear."

"Phillip, do you love me?"

He shook his head softly. "I don't know. I don't know if I can love anybody."

I nodded, tears welling up in my eyes. "Well at least you didn't say no. And because I do love you, to me that's worth fighting for. I'm not giving up on you because if I do, what does that say about me?"

He smiled. "If I die today, Rumor I can really say that someone loved me unconditionally. And that's more than a lot of people can say. But maybe you should try and let me go. To save yourself and find the love you deserve."

I heard my cell phone ringing. "I gotta take that call." I stood up and walked to the back of the bedroom. Once there I grabbed my phone and answered. "Before you say anything I'm sorry it's

110

been all night. I'll be headed over there in a little while. How's Cassandra?"

"I can't tell you over the phone."

I frowned. "What? Why not?"

"Just get here right away, Rumor. And don't make any stops. This is important."

CHAPTER ELEVEN

JONI

Cheese pulled up in front of my apartment building. I called Egan's phone again and still didn't get an answer. Frustrated, I looked over at Cheese. "You mind going inside with me?" I paused. "I know, I mean, with your brother being gone but I'm really scared to be alone with—"

"What about your nigga? How he gonna feel if he walk in on me in your crib?"

"I don't care." I looked down at my fingers as I played with them in my lap.

He nodded. "I'll walk up with you."

We got out of the car and entered my building. I was wrong on many levels for bringing him in the house but after the dude laid me down I wasn't trying to walk around by myself and it's obvious Egan wasn't here for me because he was too focused on Rumor.

Once upstairs we walked into my apartment and the first thing I smelled was shit. "What the fuck is that?" Cheese frowned.

I looked over at Milky who was sitting on the sofa, a pile of doo doo in front of him. "You know what, I'm really sick of this dog." I grabbed the dog by the collar and he growled as I drug him across the floor on the way to the door.

"Hold up, I thought you were afraid of dogs?" He asked me.

He was right and I completely forgot. "It's amazing what you can do when you're annoyed."

"Well what you 'bout to do with it?"

"What it look like? Walk him."

I grabbed him closer to the door and walked outside. He was now sniffing the ground as I looked around to be sure no one had eyes on me. When the coast was clear I let him go into the night. He must have been tired of me too because he took off running and before long He wasn't in sight at all.

When I walked back inside, Cheese looked at me suspiciously. "I picked up the shit and threw it in the trash." He frowned. "Where the dog?" He looked behind me.

"He went with one of my neighbors." I cleared my throat. "And thanks for cleaning that up too."

"I had too," he paused. "The shit was burning my nose." He washed his hands in the sink. "Well you're in the house now. You want me to bounce?"

"No!" I yelled. I realize I sounded stupid and probably like a maniac so I lowered my voice. "I mean, please don't go. Unless you really have to. I know I'm being selfish but, please don't leave me by myself."

He sighed and sat down. "I can chill for a minute but I'm not gonna be much company."

"I know and I understand." Things felt weird between us but he was still here and at the moment that's all I cared about. I sat next to him. "Can I do anything for you? Maybe make you something to eat?"

"No. I gotta burn this one out on my own." He paused, a hand over his heart. "It's just... it's just... I mean he died over dumb shit. Do you know how that makes me feel?"

I tried to touch him but he swept my hand away and I totally understood. "I'm sorry. I—"

"Let me sit alone for a second." His eyes were red and I think he was on the verge of crying. "You mind? I mean, I know this your crib."

"No, of course not." I cleared my throat. "Sure...I'm here if you need me." I got up and stuffed my hands into my back pocket. "Just going to my room, maybe clean up a little after I make a few calls."

He nodded and I walked away.

JONI

"You can't say that, Macy!" I sat on the edge of the bed to lotion my skin. I just stepped out of the shower and wanted to freshen up before bed when my brother called. "I know you say Rumor is bad but now I'm thinking that this stuff would have happened no matter what."

"How can you be sure?" He said. "Before she came into the picture your only problem was not cleaning house."

I rolled my eyes. "Macy, I wish you would stop with that dumb shit."

He giggled. "You know what I mean." He paused. "Don't even pretend to act like your house wasn't nasty. I'm gonna keep it real with you even if you don't wanna hear it."

"Right now the only thing I want is for Egan to come home. I feel like I'm stuck out here in the world alone and that ain't what I signed up for. I can't do anything until I at least know he's okay. What if those dudes laid him down too?"

"I hear all that but what you need to be worried about right now is yourself. Did he care about you when you were hit? He hit the streets again with his sister."

The door opened. " You mind if I take a shower?" Cheese asked. "I wanna freshen up a little."

I quickly put the phone down even though I know it was too late. My brother definitely heard his voice. I was sure of it. "Yeah...uh... it's down the hall."

"I hate to ask but can you give me some clean clothes?" He looked down at himself. "Got a little blood on me so I gotta burn these."

I jumped up and walked to Egan's side of the bedroom and grabbed him a fresh white T-shirt and sweatpants. It was not like he didn't let Phillip rock his gear. I was wrong on all levels but the other part of me felt good doing this type shit. Besides, he was ignoring my calls so why should I respect him. "Here...take these...they should fit."
116

He took them, nodded and walked out.

I can't lie, his sadness was killing me.

I walked back to the phone sat on my bed and picked it up. "Hello."

"Hold up! You got a man over there already?"

"Stop it, Macy."

"You trying to die a thousand deaths? What if Egan comes home and sees that man in his apartment? And you think he had a problem with me? He'll probably kill both of you!"

I sighed. "If he comes home at least I know he's okay. I don't care what he does."

"You're messing around in dangerous territory." He paused. "This from a man who can't stand your nigga. And here I thought Rumor was the only one we had to worry about. Now I find out my sister's a slut."

"Bye!" I tossed my phone on the bed.

"Aye, Joni!"

My eyes widened.

Was Cheese calling me from the bathroom?

"Joni!"

I guess he was.

Slowly I opened the door and walked down the hall and up to the bathroom door. "You...uh...you... called me?"

"Yeah. Open the door right quick so I can hear you."

I did. But stopped short of walking inside. The water was running. "Yeah?"

"No soap in here." His body was behind the red shower curtain but his face was wet. "You got some?"

I closed the door and walked to the linen closet. For some reason my body was heating up and I didn't know why. I grabbed a pink washcloth and a bar of pink Dove soap. My fingers trembled so hard I could barely hold them. Walking them back into the bathroom I placed the items on the closed toilet seat.

"You not gonna hand it to me?" He asked.

"Huh?" I responded nervously.

"The soap. I need it."

"Oh yeah!"

I fumbled with the box and removed the soap, the box floated to the floor. I was just about to hand it to him when he said, "I was wrong."

"About what?"

"When you asked if you could do anything for me I was wrong." I paused. "I kind of need a favor."

My body shook. "Okay...I...you mean...like what?"

"I think you know."

"Maybe I should go." I turned to walk away. "I have to—"

"Please, Joni. Don't go!" He paused. "I promise to be quick."

I turned back around. "I don't know about this, Cheese. I—"

"I never forgot about us and what we had, Joni. Even when—"

"You dumped me while I was in college?" I said harshly. "I loved you, Cheese. And had it not been for that I would've never gotten with Egan."

"But I loved you too!"

"And still I caught you cheating, Cheese!" I paused. "That's how you show love?"

He looked down, the water still running in the shower. "Yeah, and I'm not proud of it. I guess I took for granted that you weren't going anywhere. Guess I was wrong. You started a new life quick without me though."

"That's right. And I'm in a relationship now so it's too late."

"Let me taste it." He said ignoring my comment.

My pussy jumped. "No, I'm on my period. It's the second day but—"

"Like I give a fuck. It's still juicy."

Although my mind said no I could feel myself juicing up. He stepped out of the shower, dick stiff, big and pretty as I remembered. Not to mention it was pointing directly at me. He grabbed my hand softly and pulled me toward him. I didn't fight. I couldn't if I wanted and before long his mouth covered mine as he pressed his body against me causing us to fall into the bathroom door closing it shut.

He raised the red long t-shirt I was wearing and pulled down my white panties. Next he pushed my legs apart with his thighs, picked me up and carried me to the shower. Before I could refuse his dick pressed into the opening of my pussy and I knew I wanted him even more.

Bad.

That's probably the reason I ran into him all the time. If I needed somebody to talk to I called Cheese. If I needed someone to fight for me I called Cheese. He was then and would always be bae.

Still, this was the first time we fucked since college and now I was realizing I never got over him. You see Cheese made me scared when we were together so I went after his opposite because I didn't want to get hurt. He dressed good, kept money and had women out here circling him like sharks smelling blood.

Every day I felt like I couldn't compete. But when I got with Egan it was different. He kept a little money on him but for the most part was an average Joe. That is if you can call a low-level dope boy an Average Joe.

"I still love you," he said as water damped the back of the red shirt I was wearing and his dick stuffed into me.

"I love you too." I eased my tongue into his mouth.

"I needed this shit." He kissed me harder. "My brother... my man... is gone."

"I got you, Tony," I said calling him by his government name. "I will always be there." I bucked my hips more as he moved inside of me. We went at it for 30 minutes and when we were done we held each other closely. Until the water ran cold.

As he talked about losing his brother I looked at the door and pushed him back when I saw it was wide open. I know for a fact we closed it when our bodies pressed against it earlier so why was it open now?

Cheese was still kissing me when I placed my hand over his lips. "Cheese... didn't we... did we close that door? So why is it open?"

CHAPTER TWELVE
RUMOR

We were standing on the side of the bed where Cassandra's body sat on the floor. I just walked in and couldn't believe my eyes. When I left Dolly with Cassandra I never gave authorization for a murder. So what went wrong in the hours I was gone?

I ran my hand through my curly gold hair. "Dolly, this is not what I told you to do."

"You telling me." She smiled before putting her hands on her hips and then behind her back.

"Well what happened? Don't just sit there and say nothing."

"I killed her." She placed her hands across her chest. "I'm sorry but things got out of hand."

I frowned. " I know you killed her, bitch! But why?"

"I don't know. I was asleep and the next thing I know...um...things got out of hand." She paced a little.

"Okayyyyyyy." I threw my hands up in the air. "You gonna finish the story or not? Because right now you still saying the same thing."

"Well I'm in the bathroom and like I said I was asleep and when I woke up some kind of way she got loose and ran outside. The door was wide open and I heard her screaming for help. Her ankles and hands were still tied but some kind of way she got out of the one rope around her waist on the chair."

I sat down.

My jaw hung.

"Did...uh—"

"Nobody saw her." She said interrupting me. "So you don't have to worry about that."

I breathed a sigh of relief.

"Well at least I don't think so." She scratched her scalp. "You can never be too sure of anything I guess." She continued.

I stood up and grabbed her shoulders. "Think harder, Dolly. Did anybody see her run outside? This is serious because it could mean life or death. And you getting locked up."

She walked away and scratched her scalp again before leaning up against the wall. "There was this one car. At first I thought somebody was inside of it but it's been over an hour and the police ain't here. Guess that means we safe."

"Anything else, Dolly?" I walked up to her and pointed in her chest. "I need you to be sure!"

"I'm trying to think. Stop pushing me! I mean, you asked me to do something I've never done before. I'm not this gangster you have in your mind. I'm a hard-working woman with kids. I must've been crazy to help kidnap a person for a friend." She flopped on the edge of the bed. "I mean why would you ask me to do this? Where is your husband? He would've been way better at this than—"

"Don't make this into a situation about him." I pointed at her. "You the murderer!"

"And you a fucking kidnapper!" She said. "So what's your point? So bitch, shut up!"

I rushed up to her and smacked her in the face. Because she looked stupid I slapped her again. "This situation you got me in...no scratch that, this situation you got yourself in is serious. You are messing with my lively hood and I can't have that. If I don't get that money because you killed this girl this won't be good for anybody but especially you!"

"Are you threatening me, Rumor?"

"What you think?"

"I think right now you're scaring me."

125

"Good! Be scared! And think of a fucking way to help me get rid of this body before check-out time!"

RUMOR

I was sitting in my car trying to get a hold of my brother. When the cops came into Cassandra's apartment everything got thrown off and I forgot to go looking for him after I found Philip in an uncompromising position with a stranger. Something that I still didn't deal with yet mentally. I guess I lost my mind temporarily.

With the phone pressed against my ear I said, "Egan, I don't know where you are but I wish you fucking call me back. A lot is happening and I need your help!"

I ended the call on my cell and made another. "Hey, is Ashley home?"

"Did you call her cell first?" A man asked with an attitude.

I rolled my eyes. "If I didn't I wouldn't be calling the house. Now is she there or not?"

"You a rude bitch!"

"Look I don't have time for none of this shit. If you wanna argue with somebody go find your mama but answer my question." He laughed. Something I hated people to do when I was dead serious. "What the fuck is so funny?"

"I know about the money. And I know this is Rumor."

I sat up straight. "Who are you? And what you talking about?"

"I'm Ashley's fiancé. And I know why you keep calling and it won't help none. She not gonna tell you anything more than she already has. And she's not gonna tell you where the twins are either."

I frowned. "And why not?"

"'Cause that money is as much hers as it is yours. And when we find them, and we will find them, we won't give you a fucking dime!"

I was so mad I was trembling.

"Hello." He said. "You there?"

I hung up.

I wasn't about to say more than I already had over the phone. Besides, as far as the cops knew I was clueless about the money and the whereabouts."

I dialed Egan's phone number again. "I don't know where you are! But I need your help like yesterday!"

CHAPTER THIRTEEN

JONI

I was awakened when my face started sweating due to the sun shining through the blinds in my bedroom. When I heard something break in the living room I paused where I sat before throwing on my robe to investigate. I was surprised to see Cheese in the kitchen trying to cook breakfast and doing a horrible job at that. He agreed to sleep on the sofa last night. There was so much smoke I could barely see his face when I walked up to him.

I walked past him, snatched the pan off the stove that I believe held burnt eggs and tossed it in the sink. It sizzled loudly. "Cheese!" I looked around at the disgusting scene he made. "What you call yourself doing outside of making a mess?"

He glanced around as if he just saw how he destroyed the kitchen. "To be honest I have no fucking idea." We stared at each other and suddenly broke out into heavy laughter. "My bad, Joni. I got hungry and figured you could use a bite too. But I'll clean this up if you want." He scratched his belly and I was trying to understand that although I knew it was wrong to have him in the house, I still didn't care. Besides, Egan had yet to call me back.

I looked around. "Don't worry about it." I smiled at him. "I'm really glad you stayed though."

He shrugged. "What else I'm gonna do? I couldn't go home." He wiped his hand down his face and I could tell he was battling again with the loss of his brother. "The news mentioned earlier that my brother was murdered in what looked like a drug situation. I know everybody in my family tripping hard now. My phone been ringing off the hook non-stop." He paused. "So the last thing I want to do is be home dealing what that. Not now anyway." He sat on the sofa.

"Cheese, why did you even sell him that shit?"

He frowned. "So you blaming me for killing my own brother?"

My eyes widened. "What? No! Where did you get that from?"

"Well why bring it up at a time like this?"

I wiped my hair behind my ear. "I don't know. I'm sorry." I paused. "Guess I remembered you asking him not to smoke around you and I got
130

nosey on why you would do that." I waved the air. "Just forget I ever asked."

"First off I didn't *ask* him shit. I *told* the nigga not to smoke that shit in front of me and he did it anyway." I nodded wanting to back away from this line of questioning. "Niggas don't know how to handle that shit and—"

I put my hand on his face softly. "You don't have to tell me anything else, Cheese." I smiled. "I'm here and I can't understand what you going through right now. Please forgive me for saying the wrong things."

The front door opened and we both stood up. Egan walked inside and frowned when he looked at Cheese. "Hold up!" He paused, slamming the door. "Am I seeing things?"

"Hey, Egan, Cheese just stayed over because of what happened yesterday. With them dudes hitting me at my mama's house. Remember when I told you about the—"

"So you disrespect me in my own house?" Egan yelled moving toward us. "What the fuck is he doing here?"

Cheese laughed and kissed my cheek. "I'm out. And don't tell this nigga nothing about me and my brother."

"What you just say to me?" Egan asked following him to the door.

Cheese laughed again and walked out. While I thought his request about me not telling Egan anything about his brother getting murdered was very specific but I left it alone. Besides, I had no intentions on doing that anyway.

When the door closed I crossed my arms over my chest. "Where were you last night?" Trying to regain control of the situation that was obviously out of control. "I've been calling you all day and then you come in here like you in the right? 10:00 o'clock in the morning? I know it was wrong with Cheese but let's be realistic. This doesn't look good for either of us right now."

I walked away and he grabbed my wrist, yanking me toward him. I slapped his hand away. "Get off me! You know I hate that shit."

"And I know you, Joni." He pointed at me. "You try to pretend to be all scared but for real you sneaky as fuck."

I pointed at myself. "I'm sneaky as fuck?" I paused. "You the one who—"

"I already know what you 'bout to say and I wasn't fucking another female out here." He looked away from me. "That's the last thing on my mind."

"Yeah, you weren't fucking another female *this* time." For some reason tears rolled down my face like I was purging it all. "But what about the time I went to my family reunion that you claim you couldn't go to because you were sick?"

"Joni!"

"Only to find out you had another bitch in our house? And you wanna come at me like you all the way in the right?"

He ran his hand down his face and flopped on the sofa. He looked down and noticed the pillow and blanket where Cheese slept and looked up at me.

"That was six months ago."

"And it still hurts." I paused. "She was my best friend and I miss her to this day, even though I can never trust her again."

"Bae, all I can say is I'm sorry."

I sat next to him. "You can say more than that. How about you start by telling me where you were last night?"

"Did you fuck him?"

"If I did I would be well within my rights."

"I get all of that. But did you?" He gritted his teeth. "Because I can't see another man inside of you."

"I said no, Egan. Now where were you?"

"I don't know why but I do know you did this shit on purpose. Have this nigga in my house so I can get mad. I know you think shit is sweet because of what I did but I coulda killed that—"

The door opened again and Phillip walked inside without knocking. He looked at us and toward the back of the apartment. "Where Rumor?" Egan asked.

Philip shrugged. "I don't know, man. I thought she was here. She took me to a motel and I caught a cab this morning. What happened to you though? She was looking for you most of the night."

"Can somebody tell me what's going on?" I asked. "Please?!"

CHAPTER FOURTEEN

RUMOR

Me, Egan & Phillip sat at a table in a small diner. "I know who has the money." I said to them. "We are almost there and all of this will be over."

Egan frowned. "You not saying anything new. We all know who has the money. The twins right?"

"No," I said. Egan sat back in his seat. "Are you crazy? Then who we been chasing since you been home? Because I'm confused right now."

"I'm not one hundred percent sure but I think Ashley has it." I exhaled. "So we have to change up the plan just a little."

Egan sighed. "So it's Ashley now? First it was Cassandra and the twins. I'm starting to believe you don't know where the money is." He whispered. "You out here making wild ass moves and you going in circles. What's wrong with you?"

"Chill out."

Phillip moved around in his seat as if it were on fire. I couldn't tell if he was coming down off drugs or alcohol. I looked at him and asked, "So, so, what you want us to do, baby?"

Phillip cleared his throat. "Sit on her house. See who comes and goes. Maybe even snatch her to get her to talk if we don't see the twins." He shrugged. "To me it's a start."

Egan frowned. "Sit on her house for how fucking long?"

"For however long it takes," he said.

"I'm not gonna be able to do that." Egan told him.

"And why not?" I asked.

"Rumor, I was already out the house all night because you pulled off with my phone and wallet in the car. I had to walk three miles to my man's house. Now you want me to sit on some broad's house without even giving me an end time? I'm not feeling this at all!"

"I already told you I left because I had to find Philip."

Phillip looked down at the table.

"I get all that, but it's not my problem. He's not my problem." He paused, pointing at him. "I can't lose my girl after all of this is said and done."

I frowned. "After all of what? You getting paid? If she's a rider like you claim this should be lightweight for your relationship." Suddenly my phone rang. "Let me answer this right quick. But we're not done discussing this yet so don't leave." I pointed at him.

Egan leaned back in his seat and Phillip walked out of the diner.

"Hello?" Since this was a private call I got up from the table so Egan couldn't hear me. "I be right back, Egan. Keep that thought."

EGAN

Egan was frustrated.

First his girl had a nigga in the house and then Rumor was doing all she could to blow his world. He was all for the money but not at the expense of his life when it was all said and done. He was leaning back in the seat inside the diner when he saw something weird outside. Getting up, he went to investigate and saw Philip talking closely with some dude.

Moving nearer to them he suddenly realized exactly what was happening.

"Oh shit!" The dude said when he spotted Egan. "Is that my man, Egan?"

Egan realized at that moment that he did know him from the streets. So he shook his hand and said, "Yeah but what's this about?"

Keith looked at Phillip. "Oh, he's a head. Let me serve him right quick, bro. I'm gonna be right with—"

"Nah. You not 'bout to do that."

Keith frowned. "Wait, you know him too?"

Egan remained silent.

"I..." Keith nodded. "You know, I heard you were out the game after that nigga robbed you a while back. I'ma respect the situation now but if you walk up on another nigga fucking up his paper you could end up dead. You should—"

Egan gripped him up. "What you just say to me?"

"Nothing, man," Keith said. Egan released him. "I'll get up with you later." Frustrated, Keith walked away.

"So you a crackhead now?" Egan asked Philip. "I mean is this why you dropped the ball last night?" Philip crossed his arms over his chest and Egan had his answer. "Wow, you really fell off. Hard at that."

Philip laughed. "This from a man who fucked his girl's best friend in her own bed." Egan's eyes widened. "Oh yeah, I was listening and over her that shit too."

Egan grilled him for a second longer and stormed back to the restaurant. He wasn't about to waste any more time with him than he already had. When he made it back inside Rumor was off the call and sitting at the table. Egan stormed up to her. "Your man on that shit. Did you know that?"

Rumor looked around trying to see who overheard him.

"I asked you a fucking question." He said. "Did you know that shit or not?"

"Sit down, Egan."

"Did you?!"

"Egan, can you sit down." She yelled. "Please." Egan finally complied. "I know he's having some trouble right now but he needs me."

"You know what, I heard he was a head and a faggy back in the day but I brushed it off 'cause I ain't want nothing negative for you but now..."

"He's my husband."

"He's also a lost cause." He pointed at the table. "Don't you see that?"

"So what...you making the rules on what a real relationship looks like now? I don't care what he's on, he's mine and I'm gonna see him through all of this. And when it's all said and done everybody who didn't believe in him gonna feel real stupid too."

Egan wiped his hand down his face. "I know why you doing this. But you worth more than being with a man who can't take care of you. I mean look in his eyes, Rumor. That nigga been gone a long time ago. Rotten fruit can't turn fresh no matter how much you try and clean it. You know that right?"

She frowned. "Your girl got rid of my dog." She said. "Did she tell you that?" She pointed at him.

He sat back and clasped his hands on the table. "No she didn't. But I'm sure if she did she had a reason." He paused. "But when I asked her about it she said it ran away."

"She gonna pay for that too." Rumor paused. "Just so you know."

140

"And what does that mean? You threatening my bitch now?"

"Do you know me to make threats?" She smiled grabbed her purse and walked out of the diner.

CHAPTER FIFTEEN

JONI

When I parked my car, I saw Cheese standing in front of his mother's house. He was with his family and everyone looked sad. I started to pull off because I realized that they were in the process of burying a family member and now was a bad time to be visiting. So what was I doing here?

The moment I grabbed the gearshift to drive away his mother spotted me. "Joni, come inside!" She said waving at me. "We got a lot of food in here. Come on in and help us get rid of some of it."

JONI

"Thank you, Ms. Langston," I said rubbing my protruding belly after being stuffed with 'samples' of this and that meal. I was seated at a brown wooden kitchen table where trays covered in aluminum foil sat before me. People have been dropping food and money off all day. I could tell this family is very loved.

"No problem, Joni and thanks for the card." She placed her hand on my shoulder. "You should know it feels good to see you two friends again." She paused before looking at Cheese. "I always told him that you were the one he let get away."

"Ma..." Cheese whispered. "Stop it."

"I'm serious." She exhaled. "And after losing my son I just want my other one to be happy and—" She broke into a crying fit and ran away.

When I looked over at Cheese he was staring at the table. "Sorry 'bout that."

"Cheese, no, I totally understand."

He nodded and slowly looked up at me. The sun shining through the blinds lit up his face and made him even more attractive. "You still pretty." He said to me.

"Me?" I blushed. "That's you."

"So you calling me a female now?" He asked playfully.

"How could you be?" I giggled. "When you as fine as you are. I'm just—"

"Why you here?" He sat back in the chair and crossed his arms over his chest.

I cleared my throat. "I... I..."

"Is this 'bout your man? If so I don't want no parts of that conversation."

"What? No." I sighed. "Besides he's not my man. Not really anyway."

"What do you want from me?" He paused. "Cause I don't know if I can do all the mind playing right now. If you gonna be in the picture I need the truth."

"All I wanna do is be a friend to you right now. That's it."

"And you are." He looked out ahead. "You know it's crazy my mother still likes you so much. After all this time. What has it been? Four years?" He looked at me and touched my face. "You need to leave that dude alone, Joni."

"Don't do this, Cheese."

"Trust me, I'm not making this about me and you. He's foul, bae."

I stood up. "I gotta go."

"Do you still love me?" He asked seriously.

"Call me when you—"

He placed his hand behind the back of my head and pulled me closer to his face. Our lips almost touched. "Do you still love me? Because I still love you."

"I gotta go." I separated from him. "I'm sorry I came by." Before he could dispute I ran out the door.

JONI

I needed to get away from DC. I didn't know if it would be for a little while or forever but I knew I had to go. But first I had to come up with a plan that made sense. I walked into my living room to get the phone off the charger when I saw Rumor standing by the door. "Do you know where I was today?" She asked me.

I rolled my eyes. "I don't know and I don't care."

She extended her hand and I saw she was holding some paper. "Take it."

I frowned at her. "What is it?"

"Just look at it."

I took the paper and saw it was a picture of a dead dog in the middle of the street. It was Milky. The photo dropped from my hand and floated to the floor.

"You let him loose and that's what happened to him. Treated him like trash. Like he wasn't a living being." I saw tears welling up in her eyes and I was surprised. For some reason I thought the evil bitch wasn't capable of emotions. "No use in you lying, Joni. The neighbor told me everything. She saw you handling the dog by the collar before you let him run into the street. She didn't tell the police but she took a picture for me."

I walked over to the sofa and sat down before putting my face in my hands.

"I prefer silence then lying," She said. "It shows you have some heart."

"He was growling at me...I mean...I"

"I forgive you."

"Thank you because I didn't mean to hurt the—"

"But I need a favor." She interrupted me.

I frowned. "What kind?"

146

"I know I haven't told you a lot about why I'm here so I'll do it now."

"I'm listening..."

"I'm due money. Alot of money. And it's the reason I was arrested and did time for over 3 years. Well my charge said check fraud but that's all they could get me on."

"I'm still confused on what you want from me."

"Egan and my husband are sitting on a house right now. This girl who lives there knows where my money is and I'm going there later. But my old car has to be dumped first because the police were following me. I need a new car."

I frowned. "So why can't you do it?"

"Because I can't."

"Well that's not telling me anything?"

"Okay, well I'm picking up the money. Hopefully today. That's the reason I can't go. Now will you help me? Please? All you gotta do is dump the car in the river in Maryland." She reached in her purse and gave me an address. "This is a good place to let it roll right into the water. It's already been scouted. If you do this for me I'll give you enough money to take care of yourself forever."

"That's not important to me anymore."

She laughed. "Money is important always."

I sighed. "Well what if I say no?"

"Then I'll tell the cops about my dog. And in D.C. the law is up to five years and a $25,000 fine for that type of thing." She shrugged. "It may seem like a baseless crime but people get arrested for negligence to animals more than people know."

I lowered my brows. "So you blackmailing me now?"

"Of course not. I just really want your help."

"You'll pay for this." I pointed at her.

"I already am. Can't you tell?" She smiled and handed me a set of keys. "This is for the car and don't worry about this other key, it's for my new car. When you're done hit me on my phone." She pulled another number out of her pocket. "This is my cell phone number. After you're done place the keys back on the counter. And when I get my money I'll give you $10,000."

"Wow, you really have all of this worked out don't you." I said through clenched teeth.

"A girl gotta be prepared."

"I wish you never came into our lives."

"That's sweet, Joni but it's also a lie. It's only been days and already you look stronger than you did before I came into the picture. It's amazing what a little pressure can do for the spirit."

CHAPTER SIXTEEN

EGAN

*E*gan and Philip sat in a stolen car across from the house Rumor said Ashley lived in. Three hours passed and no one had come in or out of the premise and Egan was starting to lose major patience.

When Philip started twitching again Egan looked over at him. "You alright?"

Phillip looked at him and focused on the house again. "Like you care." He shook his head.

"You right. I don't. But I don't want you in here twitching and throwing up either."

"You act like it's your car." He paused. "But it don't even matter what you think or say. I know you hate me."

Egan laughed. "Hate is a strong word for a nigga I don't give a fuck about. To be honest I could care either which way."

Philip snickered. "You might not want to hear this but I tried to walk away from her. Just the other day but she wouldn't go."

Egan looked harder at the house when he saw someone opening a window. "Well it's obvious you didn't try hard enough."

"What you want from me, man? What you want me to do? Because even if I made a promise what's to stop me from lying about it?" He laughed. "Look at me. I'm a mess and she's all I got. That's the life of an addict."

Egan hated feeling bad for him but one thing he respected was his honesty. "I just want her safe. I want her with somebody who will bring out the best not the worst. And you gotta be honest, right now you not that guy."

Suddenly there was some movement in front of the house and they both crouched down lower in their seats. "Oh...shit there she goes!" Philip said as he unlocked the car door.

Egan grabbed his forearm. "Wait! What you doing?"

"I'ma put this to an end once and for all!" Philip ran into the street and after Ashley. She saw the crazy man and took off running screaming all the way.

Egan was surprised because although Philip was on drugs he was quick as he chased her. Instead of getting out to stop it or to help, Egan

151

followed slowly in the car. Within seconds Philip caught her by jumping on her back causing her to fall face-first to the curb splitting open her head. The street went silent again.

She died instantly.

"What the fuck you doing?" Egan asked. "Get in here!"

Philip covered his mouth with his fingers as he looked down at her bleeding body. "I'm... I'm sorry. I didn't mean to do this. I was just—" Suddenly he vomited where he stood.

"Just get in the car before I leave your ass!" Egan repeated looking around to be sure no one was watching. "Now!

RUMOR

I was sitting in the motel watching Dolly smoke her brains out when Egan called with bad news.

Ashley was dead.

Instead of being mad I grinned upon hearing the news. After all, since she wasn't giving up the whereabouts of the twins she was useless to me anyway so what did I care? Fifteen minutes later my phone rang again.

It was Ashley's man.

"I know you were responsible for this." He said. I could immediately tell from the sound of his voice that he was crying.

"Excuse me?" I sat on the edge of the bed and watched Dolly fall into ecstasy.

"No use in lying." He continued. "I know this is all you and I'm gonna let the cops know too."

I frowned. "I would like to know what you're talking about for one. I mean are you crazy or something? You called me out of the blue only to make accusations. Where's the proof?"

"My girl is gone!" He screamed.

"Well did you call her to see where she is?"

"You dirty bitch!"

I laughed. "All you had to do was get the twins information to me since you made yourself involved. If only you had, maybe Karma wouldn't come so badly on you."

"So you killed my girl because I didn't give you information?"

"Like I said, I didn't do anything!" I paused. "I have no idea what you're talking about."

"Nothing but darkness will come to you." He sniffled. "The funny part is the person who knew what you wanted to know went missing a long time ago. And you over here bothering Ashley."

"So you a preacher now?"

"It ain't about being a preacher." He paused. "But I will say that I've heard and seen this movie before. And in the end the greedy bitch always gets what's coming to her."

"So that's why your girl dead?"

He hung up and I laughed again. He could say all he wanted but he couldn't prove shit and we both knew it.

Needing a cigarette I dug into Dolly's purse and grabbed a Newport. Walking outside, I stood by the door and smoked heavily until it filled my lungs and relaxed me. All I wanted was my money so I could get Phillip help and build a life we deserved but that wasn't happening.

Now I was starting to hope that Ashley's boyfriend wasn't right.

CHAPTER SEVENTEEN

JONI

The only reason I agreed to dump the stupid car in the first place was due to guilt. No I didn't like dogs but I never wanted anything to happen to it either. So to quiet her, and prevent her from going to the police I agreed. Besides, I had been thinking of my life and the plans I had for myself didn't include guilt. So it started with righting a wrong I did to a dog. Even if I didn't like them.

My cell phone rang and I answered it. "Hey, Joni. Why you got me feeling like I can't lay my hands on you?"

I smiled when I heard his voice, but it felt differently than in the past and I didn't know why. "Hey...what you been up to?"

It was Egan and he hardly ever called so this was weird to say the least. "Not much. But I do know I miss you."

"Is that right?" I smiled. "But where are you?"

"Hold up." He paused. "You don't miss me?"

"Egan, stop it already." I made a left to merge onto the highway. "You already know how I feel
155

about you. I would think I'd be getting on your nerves as much as I tell you."

"But you feel distant since—"

"Your sister moved in with us?" I said finishing his sentence. "The past couple of days you've been so busy and I decided to just give you your space. And I guess I just been thinking about some things. On what I really want out of life."

"Bae, I know you not feeling like hearing this but I got a plan on how to get rid of her." He paused. "Just don't give up on me."

I shook my head. "Why would you need a plan when it's your house? If you don't want her there and you realize like I do that she's caused enough problems, just tell her to leave. Don't worry about the money or whatever she got going on."

"It's not as easy as you may think." He paused. "And it's not just about the money for me."

I laughed. "Then you're ruining us for free."

"Joni—"

"Joni nothing, Egan." I interrupted. "That's why I didn't want to talk about it. I'm tired of you and all of this—this—sick sibling shit you got going on with that woman. All I wanted was my relationship back. All I wanted was my man back. Can't you see that?"

"Just a little more time. That's all I need to make all this work. I got some things in motion and—"

"Please stop, Egan. You say that all the time. Besides, I don't want my mood messed up for the rest of the day."

"I love you." He said.

I shook my head.

"Joni, are you there?"

"Yes."

"Can I fuck you tonight?"

I chuckled.

"Damn. My girl laughed at me when I asked for sex? You must really be mad at me."

When I looked at the gas it was a little low. So I rolled the windows down and turned off the air to conserve it. "First of all I'm still on my period and I didn't mean to laugh." I paused and sniffed a few times. Something smelled real foul. I think I smelled it earlier but thought it was because I was driving by a dead animal or something. "Look, let's talk about sex after all this is over."

"For the record, I don't care about your period anymore. But I'll rap to you later, Joni. Maybe we can grab something to eat. And where you at anyway?"

"Egan, I gotta call you back." I hung up. He didn't know I was doing this favor for Rumor because I asked her not to tell him. Besides, I didn't need him hearing about what I did to Milky.

Focusing back on the car, the smell grew so bad it drove me crazy. And because it was hot, it made things worse. Before I drove any further I gotta find out what was up. So I pulled off the highway and onto the shoulder. Cars drove back and forth at high speeds and I knew I had to be quick.

Once the car was parked I carefully got out and opened and closed the doors checking inside. I figured some food was left in here somewhere and it was causing the smell. But after looking for about five minutes I still hadn't found anything. I was about to get back inside and make the trip to drop the car off but the oder was so horrible I couldn't do it. It was making my stomach turn. Maybe that stupid girl left food in a trunk. So I decided to check.

Using the remote I popped the trunk and looked inside. Immediately I found the smell and was so scared at what I saw I hit the ground, my ass pressing against the gravel. What was going on? And who's the dead girl inside?

Suddenly a car pulled up behind me and I knew I had to close the trunk because there was a body in it. And since I was the driver it was easy to see who they would think killed her. But my legs wouldn't move.

I was stuck!

When I looked behind me again a large man wearing blue jean overalls was approaching quickly. "Ma'am, do you need help?"

"No!" I screamed. "I mean, I'm fine. Please leave me alone!"

I caught him right before he was close enough to see what was inside. As a matter of fact if he took five more steps my secret would've been out and before long I was sure I would be in jail. Instead he stood as still as stone, staring at me. "You sure?" He asked. "Because you can hurt yourself out here like this." He looked to the left. "With the cars driving as fast as they are."

"Yes, please, I'm okay! Just go away."

"Fuck it then. That's why you can't help bitches." He said before getting back into his car and pulling off. Causing dust to swirl in the air.

That was a close call. Now I had to get my legs to move. Slowly I stood up, using the bumper as leverage. Once on my feet I slammed the trunk shut and looked around me. That dirty bitch set me up. She wanted me to drive this car probably hoping I would get caught with the body by the police. And to think, my mother warned me about her.

JONI

When the car was dumped I was staring at Egan who picked me up in front of a movie theater in the city. "I still don't understand why the cab dropped you off out here."

"I told you. He got a call about something happening to his family and he had to leave." I paused. I was still feeling shaken up a little about the person in the trunk and who it was. "About, Rumor though, I want her out tonight, Egan!" I paused. "As a matter of fact, I wanna ditch that apartment and get out of DC all together. With you."

He walked away. "I can't do either right now."

I frowned. "Why not?"

He grabbed my hand and I snatched away from him. "Bae, even if I wanted to leave I couldn't afford to go right now."

"Trust me for a change, Egan. We'll make it work." I paused. "Let's just leave now. Please, Egan." He didn't seem interested. "Either leave with me now or—"

"What I tell you about that?" He walked up to me. "Huh? Didn't I tell you not to give me no ultimatum?"

"Yes, Egan."

"Then why you keep doing it?"

"Because...because...I got something to tell you."

He looked at me seriously. "I'm listening."

CHAPTER EIGHTEEN

RUMOR

I was in front of Dolly's house waiting on the good news she claimed to have for me. An hour later she came running out of her building and I was relieved, because her lawn was filled with strange looking people who all seemed to be interested in me.

"They got them!" She said excitedly, standing on the passenger side. "Both of them!"

I put my hands on my chest. "Don't play with me like this, Dolly." I was smiling so hard I thought my face would crack and fall off. "Are you actually saying that they got the twins?"

"Yep, but you gotta have they money before they hand them over. That's one thing about my cousins, they don't play when it comes to their paper."

I waved the air. "I know! I know!"

She nodded. "This what you been waiting on. We should have gotten them on the job earlier instead of wasting so much time."

"You ain't lying. So what now?"

She sighed. "Well, they took them to the motel we were at earlier. I kept the same room you told me since we already did our thing inside of it." She looked around. "No need in people seeing us change up rooms and stuff. It's safer that way I think."

I nodded. "Good." I smiled, rubbing my hands together. "Things really coming together now. Finally shit going in my favor."

"But where the money!?" She looked around inside my car while leaning in the open window. "I wanna make sure they get it."

"I'm gonna give it to you but let me talk to them first."

She licked her lips. "You already got Fritos number. Hit him up. He expecting you."

"Oh yeah I still have it." I pulled out my cell and called the number on my new cell phone. "What's up Frito?"

"From how happy you sound, I think you already know."

I giggled. "Yeah Dolly told me you did that." I looked over at her and she was grinning like we were gonna split the paper.

"Yeah. But don't give her that though." He paused. "I don't trust her with nothing belonging to me. And you shouldn't either."

I looked at her again. "I figured as much. But I'll see you in a little while though." I tossed my phone in my purse. "Well, let me get out of here." I put the car in drive.

Dolly grabbed the door handle. "Hold up, where the money? 'Cause he wanted me to collect that. Didn't he tell you over the phone?"

Suddenly there was a dude at the driver side door trying to get inside. I didn't even see where he came from. I kept hitting the lock button even though I knew I did that before I parked. I just wanted to be sure they couldn't get inside.

"Give me the money!" Dolly screamed as she tried to slide in through the window I was rolling up.

Now I was getting nervous. One crazy was on my right the other on my left so I backed up and went forward, rolling over the foot of the person standing at my driver side. He hobbled back and I was able to get away from the scene.

I knew I didn't trust that bitch. She probably killed Cassandra because she wouldn't give her more money in the motel to buy drugs. As a matter of fact before I stuffed her in that car I checked her purse again. When I grabbed her phone to make that call to the twins the first time, she had forty dollars tucked inside. When she was dead it was gone.

It didn't matter. Because my life was about to change for the better.

I was finally getting paid.

RUMOR

I was pacing Egan's living room floor the next day. The apartment was cleaner than I remembered and figured old girl finally realized cleanliness was a must if you had a man. I was 'bout to hit Egan's phone again until the door opened." Egan, they found the twins. You have to come with me to ask him where the money is. It should only take a—"

"What did you do?" He asked with an attitude. "And no use in you fucking lying either."

I crossed my arms over my chest. "What you talking about now?"

"Joni. What did you do to her?"

I rolled my eyes and flopped on the sofa. "What did she say now? 'Cause I'm not gonna lie, the girl is starting to really work on my nerves!"

"She moved out all her fucking clothes, Rumor." He paused. "And cleaned up too. Guess it was her way of being done once and for all. If I lose her over this I'll—"

"Good," I smiled, interrupting him. "Now she's out the way. Don't you see what I'm saying? Egan, they found the twins. And right now I need your help grilling them for my money. Dolly's cousins are with them but I don't know if it's safe for me to go by myself. If we went together we could—"

"I don't give a fuck about none of that no more!" He yelled louder. "Did you or did you not set her up?"

I stood up. "So you really love her?" I paused. "Because that's got to be the reason you choosing her over me?"

"Did you put a corpse in the car you asked her to dump or not?"

166

There was no use in playing with him. I was already wasting too much time leaving Dolly's cousins alone with the twins as is. Besides, I didn't feel like lying again anyway. I was willing to say whatever I could to get away from this situation. "Yeah, I did."

"Fuck!" He placed a hand over his head. "She could have been pulled over by the cops! What if she had? Or was that your plan all along?"

"Egan, don't be crazy."

"You know what, just get out! I have done everything for you I'm able to at this point. Been by your side no matter the plan. But now I'm through. You crossed the line."

I stood up and tried to touch his hand. "Please, you my brother!"

"Cut the sneak shit out, Rumor. It's just you and me and there ain't no need in faking it anymore. We not related. We two dumb ass niggas who tried to make a little money together and failed. That's the extent of our relationship."

I smiled because I realized the hold I had over him was officially over and I always tried to save face when I was embarrassed. In the past even though we weren't related, we always referred to each other as family. And since our relationship started in grade school, most people weren't around to know we weren't really kin so they just went with what we told them.

"Wow," I said. "Guess it was good while it lasted."

"Now where is your real brother?"

"Philip is on one of his runs again. And since we're being honest he's my foster brother." I sighed. "Anyway, I'll be surprised if I see him before I get my money back."

"Your problem not mine." He opened the door. "Leave now."

I walked toward the door but stopped short of leaving. "Too much has happened for her to ever come back to you, Egan. First you chose me over her by letting me stay when she didn't want you to. Then you gave her bed and had her sleep on the sofa." I giggled a little at the thought alone. "Oh, and I made her drive the car and...well...you know the rest. Basically I'm sure she's gone forever. You sure you want me out the picture too?"

His brows lowered. "Wow... she was right about you."

I shrugged. "Can I at least get my clothes?"

"Why would I let you do that? You big money now remember?" His nostrils flared. "Now get the fuck out before I toss you out."

RUMOR

Since I couldn't find Philip and Egan dumped me, I knew I was on my own. So using the gun I owned, I pushed open the motel door, which surprisingly was already a jar. I jumped back when I realized the twins were on the bed dead. Luckily we rented the room with a fake name.

I was about to take off running when I heard, "Don't move!" Frito said sticking a gun in the small of my back from behind. "Just walk with me and you won't get hurt."

RUMOR

I handed Frito and Luke the money for finding the twins. Even though they both were dead and were of no use to me now. They were about to get out of my car when I grabbed Frito's arm. "Why kill them? I had to pay you five hundred dollars I didn't have, for nothing? At least you can do is tell me the truth."

Luke looked at Frito.

"I'ma go wait in the car," Luke said. "But hurry up. The cops could be here at any minute. We gotta bounce." He got out and slammed the door.

"I'ma be real with you, we tried to torture the money location out of them niggas. We figured we'd take the big money and well..." he laughed. "Cut you out the profits altogether. But they said something I believed."

"And what was that?"

"That Cassandra had the money all along."

"But... she... I..."

"I know," he shook his head. "She's dead. Dolly killed her." He smiled. "They told me they knew where the money was but didn't have direct access to it. And that they were only able to peel off forty grand or so since you been locked up. Something about the cops were watching them, believing you or them had the cash." He pulled a blunt from his pocket and lit it. "That's why they let you out early, to find the money which you already know. Oh, I almost forgot, they also said two cops turned dirty and for a percentage, agreed to kill you. They figured if you were dead the clean cops would stay off of their case and they could finally spend the money." He took a pull and exhaled.

Those had to be the cops who came to Cassandra's house.

"Do you know who told the police that I was involved with taking the money from the Laundromat King in the first place?" I paused. "Because I never understood how I got locked up but they didn't."

"You not gonna believe this shit if I tell you."

"Who was it?" I paused. "Phillip?"

"Nah...Egan." He took another pull and exhaled. "You better be careful in these streets because they out to get you. Good luck."

CHAPTER NINETEEN

JONI

"**M**ama, stop asking where I'm going." I said after getting up from the table when I finished eating. "Like I said earlier, I don't know yet. But when I do you'll be the first to know."

Macy walked up to us while texting on his phone.

"You know you my child right, Joni?" Mama asked me.

"Of course I do."

"So when I asked you something, you better get to answering."

I sighed. "All I can tell you right now is this...me and Egan are over."

Macy sat next to me clearly very interested. He put his phone on the sofa. "Yeah right," he said. "You say that all the time and y'all end up right back together."

"That may be true but I'm serious this time. Besides when have you ever known me to move out all of my clothes?"

"Damn," he nodded. "You are serious!"

Mama slapped him for the language. "Be careful in my house boy!" She pointed at him and farted.

"Okay, Mama." He held his face and focused on me. "Well did he call you at least? And beg you back?"

"What difference does that make?" I asked seriously. "This not a game for me. I'm not doing this hoping he'll realize what I mean to him and come running back. I'm seriously done. Before even doing this I tried to work it out and he wasn't receptive. So I gotta move on with my life because it means he wasn't the one for me. I wasted enough time as is." I shook my head. "I prayed to God for an answer earlier. I wonder with all the drama if this wasn't my answer.

"This about Rumor ain't it?" Macy asked.

"What you think?"

Mama took a deep breath and sat back placing her hand on my leg. "I know you an adult now, and I can tell by your voice that your mind is made up so I'll say this...don't leave unless you care for your loose ends. You don't want to start new only to double back. Leave with a clean slate and a clear conscience. If there's something you have to do before you go, do it. Trust me, you'll thank me for it later."

JONI

Cheese was dressed in all black when he stepped out his car in front of his house. The funeral was earlier today and he looked sad which was to be expected. But for some reason he smiled when he saw me. "Damn, didn't expect to see you again after the way you left," he said in a low voice. "But how you doing?"

"I should be asking you." I said in a low voice, looking downward.

He shrugged. "Today was hard." He looked back at his house. "I can't even lie. Especially on my mother, but we gonna be okay. This our way of life now ain't nothing we can do about it. At the end of the day my brother is gone. Forever."

I nodded. "I broke up with him."

"Whoa." His voice sounded really concerned. "How he take it?"

"I don't even care. I wanted all loose ends cut before I came here. To see you."

He smiled a little. "Word?"

I smiled. "Come with me, Cheese."

"Where we going?" He asked.

"Does it matter?" I grabbed his hand.

"Nah, Mommy." He kissed me gently on the lips. "I could use the escape."

JONI

Cheese and me were lying in a high-end hotel after having sex. He was smoking a blunt when he said, "When you said you had a room I thought it was something smaller." He paused. "But the Ritz Carlton in the city?"

I giggled. "You like?"

"Yeah. At first all I was thinking about was..." he slipped his finger into my pussy. I was off my cycle and was glad because we fucked all over this room. "This warm box."

I grinned. "Yeah, it was nice. I almost forgot how good we are together."

He removed his finger. "Even after the shower thing the other day?" He paused. "But look, those niggas who shot at us in the car, they were after Roland. He had been smashing one of their kid's mothers and wanted blood."

I almost forgot about that but part of me was glad it happened. It put us back together. I smiled but then grew serious. "Well, I have another question I want the answer too. Why did you leave quickly when Egan came home that day? I've never known you to run from anything, especially not another man but you looked shook."

"It wasn't obvious?" He paused. "We just fucked in your man's crib, I was in the kitchen cooking breakfast and the nigga came home. Where's the mystery in that? It's clear cut right?"

"No, Cheese. Something felt different. I've known you too long."

He sighed. "Alright, alright. If we gonna do this over I don't wanna start with lying to you. Your man was wired."

177

"Huh? I don't understand."

"I don't know why because I was clear. When he came home that day he was wearing a wire and I saw it through his T-shirt."

I covered my mouth.

"When I went asking around, I heard he was informing on his own crew, which is why he got robbed not too long ago. Apparently he got busted a while back while slinging and in order to stay out of prison he turned snitch. That's why I told you not to tell him anything about what happened when my brother was killed." He continued. "Now let me ask you a question. Who opened that bathroom door when we were in the shower?"

I moved uncomfortably on the bed. Not only because of his question but also because the idea that Egan was working with the police was too hard to believe. "Uh...nobody came to the bathroom. I told you that already. I just forgot to close the door."

"The thing is, Joni, I don't believe you. You left the bathroom and didn't come back for fifteen minutes. I heard you whispering to somebody in the living room. Now if you wanna be with me you gotta be real too because I need the truth."

"I was on the phone and—"

"Joni, I'm 'bout to bounce." He paused. "I understand you different now. I can see it in your eyes. Back in the day I couldn't even go get carryout food and leave you in the house without you losing your mind." He chuckled. "So don't add lying to the new you."

I swallowed hard and stood up. Then I walked to his side of the bed, clasped my hands in front of me and looked over at him. "If I tell you this…if I say what I'm about to, you can't tell nobody."

"If you gotta say all that, keep it to yourself because it means you don't trust me."

I exhaled. "The person who came to the door gave me money. And a lot of it too."

THE DAY THE DOOR WAS OPENED

Joni closed the bathroom door where Cheese was still waiting inside, and walked to the living room to investigate. Her heart pounded as she hoped Egan hadn't caught her in a very uncompromising and sexual situation. When she got to the living room she saw a short older woman holding an orange duffel bag.

"Who are you?" Joni asked tugging her robe closed. "And what are you doing in my apartment? How did you get in here?"

"The door." She said in a low shaky voice. "It was...open. I just let myself inside." Suddenly she wept and placed a free hand over her mouth. "I'm sorry. I don't mean to drop all of this on you but I...I just...want my daughter back."

"Your daughter back?" Joni stepped closer not understanding the question. "Who is she?"

"Cassandra."

"I—"

"Look, I already know you have her so no use in lying." The woman extended her palm with her hand in her direction. "There's the money." She paused. "Most of it is there anyway. We only used about $40,000 over the years." She wiped tears from her eyes. "I'm talking about me, my daughter, and the twins. Mostly for bills and stuff like that. But the rest is all there." She paused. "Now please

I'm begging you, wherever my daughter is, let her go, Rumor. She's all I got." She walked out.

JONI

BACK IN THE ROOM

Cheese stared at me after hearing the story. "That's why you wanted to leave. So you can get away in case they looking for it." He paused. "So you... you still got that?"

I nodded yes. "I know it's wrong but Rumor was so mean to me and I had been praying for a way to start all over. When she dropped the money on the floor I figured my prayers were answered. Stranger things have happened right?" I asked with wide eyes. "Plus Rumor did something real mean, Cheese. She had me driving a car with a body inside and I think it was Cassandra. As far as I'm concerned she owes me the money."

"Wow...that could've went a whole lot of different ways. With you transporting a dead body you had no hand in killing. I'm glad you still here to talk about it."

"Me too." I paused. "Still wanna be with me?" I asked.

"What you think?"

I hugged him tightly.

CHAPTER TWENTY

RUMOR

I was broke.

Homeless and Phillip was gone.

Not in death although I would have preferred it that way, but to the streets. After a week of hiding and coming to the realization that I would never get the money, I decided to find my husband. I figured with a little prayer we could work on each other. I finally located him in a crack house where a man had him bent over a wooden spool while he sexually assaulted him from behind. What is up with him and anal sex?

Well, maybe that's too rough.

He basically was having sex for money and drugs. But after running the man away with my gun, I helped Phillip to his feet. He could barely stand up and lost more weight then he had from when I saw him last. All I could do was cry silently.

I walked over to him. "You're coming with me!" I grabbed him by the arm. "I'm not leaving you in this place." The man hustled out of the room.

He hit my hand. "Who are you?"

I frowned, my heart rocking in my chest. "Phillip, it's me! Your wife!"

"Well I don't know you! And all you did was mess up my money just now!" He walked further away from me while pulling up his clothes. "Now I gotta find somebody else to help me."

"Philip, please just—"

"Go! I want you to be gone! Now!"

"Philip, I—"

"What is wrong with you? Why can't you understand that I'm not the same person?" He picked up a brick and tossed it at me. It missed my head by inches. "Now go!"

Huge tears rolled down my face as I backed up toward the door. I kept my eyes on him the whole time, hoping he would change his mind. When it hurt too much to look at his face I turned around and touched the doorknob.

"Rumor."

My heart stopped when he called me and I turned around slowly and faced him again. "Yes, Phillip."

"Stuff didn't go your way." He looked downward. "And I know you can't see it now but maybe that's a good thing." He paused. "You gotta learn to start all over, even if that means with

184

new people. In a new place." He exhaled. "I love you but you gotta let me go. Don't come looking for me again. Okay?"

I nodded, turned around and ran outside.

Now I was officially alone.

No money.

No brother.

No husband.

And no friends.

Even Dolly was out of my life since she tried to rob me. There wasn't a bright side at all for me and I felt I would be better off in prison.

Devastated, I got into my car, preparing to hit the road to somewhere when I was suddenly pulled over by the cops. "What do you want?" I said to myself. I immediately put my gun under my front seat.

The officer parked, got out and pulled up on me. "License and registration please."

I opened the glove compartment and quickly gave it to him. "Is something wrong?"

He looked at me and walked away. Twenty minutes later he briskly approached the car. "Get out and place your hands on top of your head!" He retrieved his weapon and pulled it on me. "NOW!"

"What is this about?" I got out and he slapped the handcuffs on me. "What did I do?"

"All you need to know now is that you coming with me!"

"Do you have a warrant? Because I know my fucking rights."

"I most certainly do. We have questions about the disappearance of Cassandra Avery."

He pushed me to the squad car, opened the door and shoved me in the back seat. My heart banged within the walls of my chest. "But I didn't do anything," I said half truthfully. At the end of the day Dolly killed her not me.

"Tell it to the judge."

When the door closed I heard him on the radio calling more officers, letting them know they found me. When they arrived they searched the inside of my vehicle. They found my gun. I knew I was toast but when they popped the trunk, four officers surrounded it and looked shocked at what they were seeing. I was clueless because as far as I knew nothing was there. Before long the officer who arrested me removed a severed hand and glared at me.

Wow.

I guess Joni wasn't as dumb as I thought.

EPILOGUE

E *gan just left court after testifying against his friends in a drug conspiracy case. He had been an informant for over a year and had no idea that people were on to him, which was why his money was lacking. The main defendant admitted to killing several people in drug related crimes and was handed down a sentence of life without parole. This verdict came two weeks after Rumor's trial where she was sentenced ten years for kidnapping while Dolly was given fifty years for murder.*

While driving down the street, all of his luggage in the back due to having to leave town because he was a known snitch, he thought about Joni and how he let her get away. If only he could take back time he could've been happy with her.

When he came to a stop sign he glanced to his right and so a couple kissing in a red BMW. When their lips separated, he was stunned to see it was Joni and Cheese. Shocked, when he glanced at her ring finger he saw a fat rock, which indicated she was married.

When Joni glanced over she saw Egan staring in her direction. Instead of being angry with him, she smiled. After all, Rumor coming back into the picture brought her back to the one she always loved. Not only that, but she and Cheese had both gone back to college for business management after having been married for six months. They were opening a pizza parlor in Georgetown, a suburb of Washington D.C.

When their eyes met Egan winked.

And when the light turned green they both went their separate ways.

Forever.

The Cartel Publications Order Form

www.thecartelpublications.com
Inmates **ONLY** receive novels for $10.00 per book.
(Mail Order **MUST** come from inmate directly to receive discount)

Shyt List 1	_____	$15.00
Shyt List 2	_____	$15.00
Shyt List 3	_____	$15.00
Shyt List 4	_____	$15.00
Shyt List 5	_____	$15.00
Pitbulls In A Skirt	_____	$15.00
Pitbulls In A Skirt 2	_____	$15.00
Pitbulls In A Skirt 3	_____	$15.00
Pitbulls In A Skirt 4	_____	$15.00
Pitbulls In A Skirt 5	_____	$15.00
Victoria's Secret	_____	$15.00
Poison 1	_____	$15.00
Poison 2	_____	$15.00
Hell Razor Honeys	_____	$15.00
Hell Razor Honeys 2	_____	$15.00
A Hustler's Son	_____	$15.00
A Hustler's Son 2	_____	$15.00
Black and Ugly	_____	$15.00
Black and Ugly As Ever	_____	$15.00
Year Of The Crackmom	_____	$15.00
Deadheads	_____	$15.00
The Face That Launched A	_____	$15.00
Thousand Bullets		
The Unusual Suspects	_____	$15.00
Miss Wayne & The Queens of DC	_____	$15.00
Paid In Blood (eBook Only)	_____	$15.00
Raunchy	_____	$15.00
Raunchy 2	_____	$15.00
Raunchy 3	_____	$15.00
Mad Maxxx	_____	$15.00
Quita's Dayscare Center	_____	$15.00
Quita's Dayscare Center 2	_____	$15.00
Pretty Kings	_____	$15.00
Pretty Kings 2	_____	$15.00
Pretty Kings 3	_____	$15.00
Pretty Kings 4	_____	$15.00
Silence Of The Nine	_____	$15.00
Silence Of The Nine 2	_____	$15.00
Prison Throne	_____	$15.00
Drunk & Hot Girls	_____	$15.00
Hersband Material	_____	$15.00
The End: How To Write A	_____	$15.00
Bestselling Novel In 30 Days (Non-Fiction Guide)		

Upscale Kittens	_____	$15.00
Wake & Bake Boys	_____	$15.00
Young & Dumb	_____	$15.00
Young & Dumb 2:	_____	$15.00
Tranny 911	_____	$15.00
Tranny 911: Dixie's Rise _____		$15.00
First Comes Love, Then Comes Murder _____		$15.00
Luxury Tax	_____	$15.00
The Lying King	_____	$15.00
Crazy Kind Of Love	_____	$15.00
And They Call Me God	_____	$15.00
The Ungrateful Bastards	_____	$15.00
Lipstick Dom	_____	$15.00
A School of Dolls	_____	$15.00
Hoetic Justice	_____	$15.00
KALI: Raunchy Relived	_____	$15.00
Skeezers	_____	$15.00
You Kissed Me, Now I Own You	_____	$15.00
Nefarious	_____	$15.00
Redbone 3: The Rise of The Fold	_____	$15.00
The Fold	_____	$15.00
Clown Niggas	_____	$15.00
The One You Shouldn't Trust	_____	$15.00
The WHORE The Wind		
Blew My Way	_____	$15.00
She Brings The Worst Kind	_____	$15.00

(**Redbone 1 & 2** are **NOT** Cartel Publications novels and if **ordered** the cost is **FULL** price of $15.00 **each**. **No Exceptions**.)

Please add $5.00 **PER BOOK** for shipping and handling.

The Cartel Publications * P.O. BOX 486 OWINGS MILLS MD 21117

Name: _____

Address: _____

City/State: _____

Contact/Email: _____

Please allow 5-7 BUSINESS days before shipping.

CPSIA information can be obtained
at www.ICGtesting.com
Printed in the USA
LVOW03s1505220218
567559LV00001B/182/P